Taggart

FEAR

Taggart knew what it was to be frightened, for he had seen frightened people before, and this girl was not gasping at shadows. She knew the Apaches. She had been a child when they had taken her, and she had survived. But now she was a woman, and she had seen what they did to women.

But how could she ask Taggart to stay, when asking him to stay was the same as asking him to die? Taggart grinned grimly to himself. She wasn't the only one who was afraid . . .

Louis L'Amour

Taggart

CORGI BOOKS
A DIVISION OF TRANSWORLD PUBLISHERS LTD
A NATIONAL GENERAL COMPANY

TAGGART

A CORGI BOOK 552 08486 7

First publication in Great Britain

PRINTING HISTORY
Corgi edition published 1960
Corgi edition reissued 1970
Corgi edition reprinted 1972

This book is set in 10 pt. Times

Corgi Books are published by Transworld Publishers Ltd.,
Cavendish House, 57-59 Uxbridge Road,
Ealing, London, W.5.
Made and printed in Great Britain by
Hunt Barnard Printing Ltd., Aylesbury, Bucks.

Chapter 1

Adam Stark was three months out of Tucson when he found his first color. It appeared as a few scattered flakes of gold dry-panned from the base of an alluvial fan, but the gold was rough under the magnifying glass.

Gold that has washed any distance from its source becomes worn and polished by the abrasive action of accompanying rocks and gravel, so this gold could not be far from its point of origin.

With caution born of hard experience, he seated himself and lighted his pipe. A contemplative man by nature, experience had taught him how Man may be deluded by hope, and so he smoked his pipe through, considering all aspects of the problem.

He was in the red heart of Apache country, some miles from the nearest white man and beyond any possibility of help if attacked. He was forty-four years old, with a Mexican wife and an unmarried sister, and both were in camp close by.

In Tucson they thought him insane for taking women away from town with Apache trouble always imminent, but he had neither a place to leave them nor means of supporting them during his absence. Nor did he wish to leave his wife behind. Miriam was another story, for she had a mind of her own. That was one of the reasons she was still unmarried, although she'd had more chances than most.

Adam was not sure why Miriam had joined them, but no doubt she had her reasons. During the years since their childhood he had come to possess a considerable respect for the quality of her judgment . . . yet she often startled him with her sudden decisions. There was between them more than the natural affection resulting from relationship. They were good friends also, each appreciating the qualities of the other.

The gold he panned had been taken from a spot on that alluvial fan which left small doubt that the source lay higher up the mountain, for there was no other way the gold could have reached the place where he had discovered it.

Two further pans taken from higher up the fan confirmed his belief, convincing him that if he could not find the lode from which this gold had flaked off, he could make a stake placering the debris from the fan itself.

Yet every moment they were in danger, and if discovered by Apaches they would surely be killed. Nonetheless, the quest for gold had brought him here, and he meant to have what he had found. The women were in even worse danger than he, but they had elected to come along. . . . Moreover, Adam Stark was a man who knew his own strength, his own capabilities, and he felt that with reasonable care he could keep his presence here unknown.

His reasons for wanting the gold were two. He wanted the gold to buy and stock a ranch for himself and his wife, and he wanted the gold so that he might take Consuelo to San Francisco and give her the taste of luxury and easy living she seemed so much to want.

For himself the desert was enough, the desert and that ranch and the freedom it offered. But he enjoyed the giving of pleasure to others, and to Consuelo whom he loved, he could not give too much. Adam Stark knew himself thoroughly, and he knew that his wife did not know him. Despite the fact that she now insisted she no longer loved him, he was sure she was mistaken, and he did love her. She had wanted a more obviously strong man, one with flash and demonstration. He suspected that Consuelo accepted the appearance of strength for its reality . . . and there was considerable difference. Adam had been in love with her from their first meeting, but he had been amazed when she accepted him.

Miriam . . . he was never sure what it was Miriam wanted of life, but he was sure Miriam knew and that was all that mattered. A man was part of it, but a man for Miriam must be stronger than she, and she was a strong woman. He would have to be a lot of things, and Miriam was not one to accept less than her desires.

Adam Stark turned his thoughts to the immediate problem. Their supplies, if augmented by game and what herbs they could gather, would last them, at most, two months. Connie knew the plants the Indians used for food, and whatever faults she might have, she was not lazy. She was, as old Fritz at Tucson had said, "a lot of woman."

The first requirement was shelter, a place of concealment, relatively close to water; and the second thing was to eradicate, so far as possible, the tracks left by their wagon and horses and mules. And then he must establish a pattern of operation.

Adam Stark was a man of method, and half of his success here would result from proper habits of work and movement. He must plan for their protection and their food, and for getting out the gold itself. It was too easy to become careless, and to become careless in the desert, in Apache country, meant one would die suddenly.

The desert can be a friendly place, but the rules of life in the desert are harsh, calling for understanding of certain fundamentals. Without that understanding, death could come quickly from heat, from thirst, from exhaustion, from rattlesnakes or Apaches. The rule of desert survival was to live *with* the desert and not against it, for all desert life is an accommodation to conditions that exist.

Rising from the place where he sat, Adam Stark climbed Rockinstraw Mountain.

It was the highest point in many miles. To the west the great mesas of Redmond Mountain and Squaw Peak dominated the landscape, but neither was as high as the mountain upon which he took up his position.

To the northwest and just beyond the Salt River was the ominous-seeming bulk of Black Mesa. To the north, and less than three miles away, the Salt River took a deep horseshoe bend into which several dry washes opened.

The western approaches to his position were walled off by the mesas except for two gaps, through one of which the Salt River flowed. To the east the country was broken by many canyons, most of them small, but from the top of Rockinstraw an observer could study most of the country in that direction. He started to turn away when his eye caught an odd shape among the canyons to the east, and not far off.

Getting out his field glasses, over the end of which Stark had arranged a hood of stiff leather to prevent the sun from reflecting off the glass, he directed them at the canyon where he had seen that odd, straight-edged rock.

The canyon itself was narrow, scarcely more than a wide crack in the earth, and nondescript in appearance, but from his place on top of the mountain he could see what appeared to be not a rock but the edge of a roof, and beyond it something that might be a church tower.

He was suddenly excited. It was absurd, but there were stories of the Lost Mine of the Padres supposedly somewhere in this area. The Southwest was filled with stories of lost mines, and most of them pure myth, yet there was gold here, and this was supposed to be the proper area . . . although it might be anywhere in a vast region several hundred miles square, some of the roughest country in the world.

It was typical of Adam Stark that he remained where he was until he had carefully checked the country around for any movement, any smoke, any sign of Indians. The more he studied the terrain from this vantage point, the more he realized that this must be the lookout they would continue to use.

Few would suspect a lookout on top of Rockinstraw, and from here almost the entire country could be searched. If either white men or Apaches were seen approaching, all activity at the camp or the mine workings would cease until the strangers were gone from the vicinity.

There were springs below the mountain. He located Sycamore Spring, of which an Apache friendly to white men had told him several years before, and he found what must be Mud Springs, of which he had also heard.

Taking careful sightings and establishing landmarks from the top of the mountain, he went down, mounted his horse, and began his search. Yet even after locating the canyon from the top of the mountain, it took him more than an hour to find it, so hidden was it.

It required another hour to find a way to descend into

the canyon, but by that time he had decided. This was to be their home.

There was a tiny chapel, only large enough to seat ten or twelve persons, and there was a long building constructed of stone slabs and roofed with cedar timbers. There was also an adobe stable, partly in ruins. Nearby was an *arrastra* where the ore had been broken up to extract the gold.

Ghostly silence gripped the canyon. No sound could be heard but the soft footfalls of his horse as he rode along the canyon in the sandy bottom.

He dismounted and went into the long house. Pack rats had nested here, an owl slept on a low beam. The house was still dry, compact, perfect.

Beyond the chapel in a corner of rocks he found a trickle of water falling into a basin some six feet in diameter. It was good water, clear, cold, and sweet.

The following day Adam Stark brought his wife and sister to the canyon and they moved in. The wagon he concealed in the brush some three miles away, and covered it with brush in a clump of prickly pear.

Miriam Stark put the bucket under the trickle of water and then straightened to wait until the bucket was full, shading her eyes toward Rockinstraw Mountain. It was time for Adam to be returning.

In the three weeks they had lived in the canyon only Adam had been to the diggings, and when either of the women suggested going, he persuaded them to forget it for the time being. Each day he returned with a sack or two of ore which he broke up for the highgrade they contained. He had found the mother lode . . . the very gold for which this settlement had been constructed, but which the padres themselves had never found.

Methodical as always, Adam Stark devoted four hours each day to mining, and four hours to hunting or searching for food; the remainder of the time he gave to work around the canyon itself. In all his movements he was careful to avoid using the same route or leaving any tracks. Some part of each day was spent studying the country and its approaches from the top of Rockinstraw.

Often that was done by Miriam, who had come to love the place and the far horizons it offered. Their brief periods of observation were not fool-proof. It was still possible for an enemy to approach the area without being seen, during a time when no watcher waited on top of the mountain. However, this would not be easy to do, for the possible approaches could be studied with care, and most of them could be covered to such an extent that a traveler could be seen when still far away.

Miriam was a tall girl who stepped out in easy strides and had never known what it was to be tired from walking. At twenty-eight she was of an age to be considered an old maid by everyone but herself, but to herself she felt no older than she had at twenty, and the fact that she was unmarried worried her not in the least.

Long ago she had decided that marriage was not worth the trouble if one was married to any but the right man, and she was content to wait. The passing of years since she was sixteen had not dimmed her enthusiasm in the least.

Several times men whom she respected had wished to marry her, and once she had even met a man more exciting than she would have wished, but she had good sense enough to know he was the wrong man, and he like the others had been sent away.

Shading her eyes toward Rockinstraw she saw no sign of Adam, although it was about this time, at the end of his day, that he went to the peak for a last look around the country before dark. She knew just where on the mountain to look for him, though there were plenty of other places too on the mountain which offered concealment, and even some caves that had once been inhabited by cliff-dwelling Indians. Tonight there was no sign of him.

When the bucket was filled she carried it back to the house. Consuelo was preparing supper.

"You see him?"

"No . . . he's probably on his way back."

"You think what we do if he does not come back? Suppose somebody kill him? What we do then?"

"We would saddle up and ride to Tucson."

"I think 'Paches come here," Consuelo said gloomily. "I feel it. We are fool to stay."

6

"You wanted to go to San Francisco and buy a lot of fancy clothes . . . that was all you talked about in Tucson, so what did you expect him to do? He loves you."

"He is fool."

"Any man is a fool who will waste time on a woman who does not love him, and you don't love Adam. He ought to take you back to Tucson and leave you there."

"He is weak. He is frighten. Once . . . once I think I love him, but I like a strong man. Adam is not strong."

"Adam has a sort of strength you'll never understand, Connie, and he has gentleness, too. I hope the day comes when you realize the sort of man you married. He's worth a dozen of that trash you seem to think are strong . . . like Tom Sanifer."

Consuelo's eyes flashed. "You know why Adam bring me here? Because he was 'fraid I run off with Tom Sanifer, that's why . . . and he was right. If Tom had come back I would have gone where he asked me. Tom told Adam when he came back he'd take me away."

"In front of you?"

"Yes . . . he told him. Adam, he just stand there and say, 'I think you won't do that.' Adam is a coward. If he is not a coward he would shoot Tom Sanifer then. He would shoot him dead, and then I love Adam. But he does nothing, he just looks at Tom and he say, 'I think you not do that.'"

"What happened when Tom came back?"

"He did not come back before you came, and then Adam bring us here. He bring us here because he is afraid that I will go with Tom."

"You don't know your husband, Connie. Adam was not afraid. That is his way, and if you two are to be happy you must understand that . . . you are Latin, and your people are demonstrative. Adam is not."

Consuelo turned sharply around. "I do not care! You think I want to live all my life in the desert? I am woman! I want to have happiness! I want music, good food to eat, place to go! I want to dance, to sing, to be glad! There are men who will give me what I want."

"And after?"

"Who thinks of after? He has gold now . . . why don't we go? Why does he wait until we are all dead?"

Miriam was folding the clothes she had washed. "In some ways," she said quietly, "I think Adam is a fool. If he had used good sense he would have let you go with that man, and be glad that you were gone."

"Oh?" Consuelo turned on her angrily. "What do you know about man? I think you never have a man. I think you don't know what to do with one if you have him."

"Maybe I wouldn't," Miriam agreed, "but I could give it a try."

"You afraid of man. You afraid of what man do to you. I like a strong man, who wants a strong woman. I think Tom Sanifer was like that."

"From what they told me in Tucson, Tom Sanifer was a cheap bully in a loud shirt."

"You hear lie. He was a strong man . . . a big man."

Miriam wiped off the table top and began placing dishes for the evening meal. She had never known much about the relationship between Connie and her brother. Adam was not inclined to discuss his personal affairs, but she had guessed he was not happy. However, she was equally aware that he loved the girl he had married, and if Adam loved her that was enough for Miriam.

"I think you don't like me," Consuelo said suddenly. "I think you hate me."

Miriam considered it, and then shook her head. "I don't hate you. I might even like you if you weren't married to Adam, but he deserves better than you're giving him."

"Does he complain? Does he think I am not enough woman?"

"There's more to being a woman than what happens with a man in bed, believe me. You should learn that. What you can give a man in bed he can get from any street woman, what he wants from a wife is that, but much more. He wants tenderness, understanding, the feeling of working together for something. You're stealing from him, Connie."

"I? Steal?"

"You're robbing him of that. If you don't give him more than you're giving him now, you're not a wife, you're a whore."

"So? You know nothing."

8

"He should have let Tom Sanifer have you. You'd have been better for him . . . he'd probably want nothing more from you."

"Some day," Connie straightened and her eyes flashed, "some day I think I kill you."

"You won't kill me. You won't even try, Connie, because if you did I'd kill you. You might kill Adam because he loves you, but you won't kill me, and you won't even try."

"You think."

Boots scraped on the gravel outside and Adam Stark came in the door, smiling. "It was a good day," he said, "the best yet."

"Supper's ready."

He stood for a moment in the door looking around the room. It was unbelievable to him that so bare a place could have been made to look so much like a home, and with so little to do with. And it was home. Sometimes he was afraid he would never know any home but something such as this, and he wanted the good things of life for Connie and for himself.

Considering it, he realized that somehow he never worried about Miriam, and that was wrong. He did not worry about her because she seemed so self-sufficient, so strong. She was like their mother had been, only more so, much more so. But he felt it was wrong to think of a girl that way . . . it was wrong for any man to consider a girl self-sufficient, for men wanted to do something for a woman, and when there was nothing they could do, there was no place for love.

Love was, he suspected, much a matter of service. One loved and was loved, as one needed and was needed. Or so it seemed to him.

Shadows were filling the canyon, and only the sky was bright. The canyon in which they lived was from thirty to sixty feet wide through much of its length. Only where the buildings stood was it a bit wider, but even there it seemed no wider, for the buildings were partly protected from above by the overhang of the cliffs.

Except from that one point at the top of Rockinstraw, there was no way of seeing into the canyon, and the edges of the canyon were concealed by a scattered growth of prickly pear, ocotillo, and juniper, with here and there some scattered pin oaks.

"Stay home tomorrow," Consuelo suggested suddenly.

"No." Adam Stark drew back a home-made chair. "There's work to do. Every day I don't dig makes it a day more we have to stay . . . so I'd rather work."

"Aren't you thinner?" Miriam asked. There were hollows in Adam's cheeks she had never seen before.

He smiled. "A man with two women . . . they fuss too much. Sure, I may be thinner. This is a hot country, and swinging a pick isn't the way to put on beef."

"Did you see anything from the mountain?"

Adam finished the mouthful of food he had taken and filled his cup before replying. "I'm not sure," he said. "I thought once I saw a flash over north of here . . . like sunlight on a rifle barrel, but nobody would be up in that country."

"You've been there?"

"Hunting . . . there's nothing over there."

"Did you see it again? That flash, I mean?"

"No."

"But you think it was somebody? You think someone was over there?"

"Maybe . . . it was sudden, then gone. Might have been the sunlight on a sliding rock, or something."

"You don't believe that?"

"No," he replied honestly, "I don't."

"I am not afraid," Consuelo said, and seated herself at the table. "I can shoot."

Chapter 2

Swante Taggart was still alive. Under a copper sky he rode his horse through a rust and copper land. Through time-corroded hills flecked with the green of juniper or the dusty gray of sage he walked the gaunt steeldust, knowing the ache of hunger and the heaviness of nights without sleep.

At thirty-two, Swante was thankful for the years behind and hopeful for those yet to come, but now he lived, not from day to day, or even from hour to hour, but from minute to minute.

That he rode through such a land at such a time was a matter of selection but not of choice. The choice had been made for him by the sudden arrival of Pete Shoyer at Crown King.

The selection of route was Swante's own, for he knew it well enough to doubt anyone would follow him . . . but Shoyer was doing it.

Eleven of the posse had turned back when Swante Taggart had ridden into Apache country, but Shoyer was behind him, and there were still men with him, although but few.

Taggart was out of water, out of food. Somewhere south of him was Globe, but he did not want to go to Globe. And he was at least three hard days' ride from the mining town of Morenci. Three days or even more at the rate of travel he must use, for Geronimo's dust-brown warriors were riding a grudge against the white man, and under cover of Geronimo's activities a dozen small bands had come out to raid and kill.

No ridge could be crossed without a careful study of the country around, and he must take time to hide his own trail when that was at all possible. A dozen times already he had doubled and changed direction, but so far he had been less than lucky, for Pete Shoyer was still behind him.

Pete Shoyer was a man-hunter by choice and profession. He had been a scout for the Army, as had Taggart himself, and they had known each other slightly, but without liking. Shoyer had also ridden as a paid gunhand for the big cattle outfits, and lately he had been a Wells Fargo agent and a deputy United States marshal. Taggart did not mean to be taken, and Shoyer was notorious for bringing in dead men, but until now Swante Taggart had never fired a shot at a man wearing a badge, and he did not want to begin . . . even with Pete Shoyer.

The Verde River and twenty miles of blistering land lay behind him, but by the route Taggart had taken he had covered more than thirty miles. Leaving the Verde he had taken what he believed was Canyon Creek trail, but it had proved a cul-de-sac north of Lion Mountain. When he found a way out of there and reached the bed of Alder Creek, the sand was dry and there was no hint of water, anywhere.

When he got down now from the horse he staggered, and for a moment he leaned against the horse before straightening to look around. He had drawn up in the partial shade of a thick clump of juniper, and squinting his eyes against the glare, he searched the country before him.

Five miles away and three thousand feet lower was Tonto Creek, a faint green line indicating its course. Beyond the valley of the Tonto, the Sierra Anchas were a wall across the sky. Taking his time, fighting the weakness brought on by thirst, hunger, and exhaustion, Swante Taggart worked out a course that would take him to the old Apache trail that lay alongside Greenback Mountain and toward the peak of Lookout, which lay beyond.

To the south, at least twenty miles away, the Four Peaks of the Mazatals bulked dark against the sky.

If there was no water in Tonto Creek, he must try for Turkey Spring, and once in the canyons of the Cherry Creek country Shoyer would never find him. He knew that country.

But he was fooling himself if he believed he would get farther than the Tonto without water. If there was no water there, he would do as well to make a stand there, for he would die anyhow. His horse would go no further than the Tonto . . . if he made it that far. And a man without a horse in this country was a dead man.

Nothing moved but the wind. His hand carelessly brushed a rock exposed to the sun, and it burned like a red-hot iron. His eyes searched the desert again. He should be moving on, yet he was reluctant to stir, and when at last he started to mount, he stopped, frozen in place.

Not two hundred yards away an Apache warrior sat a spotted pony.

Swante spoke softly to his horse and waited, holding very still, for to move was to be seen.

The Apache started his pony and walked it slowly forward, crossing the very trail Taggart would have taken had he gone forward at once. And had he gone on without stopping, the Apache would now be on his trail, for his tracks would have been seen.

He heard the movement before he saw them, and when they came up out of the juniper and ocotillo along the slope there were at least forty of them, including children and squaws. No less than seventeen were fighting men.

Holding his breath, he waited, careful not to look directly at them for fear he might draw their attention. They moved slowly, for with them was a travois with a sick or wounded man upon it.

When they had gone by he sat down on a rock in the shade and waited there for what might have been twenty minutes. When he did start moving he walked beside the steeldust to lower the silhouette they would make against the sky.

No sound disturbed the blazing afternoon. He was sodden with weariness and weaving as he walked. Behind him the led gelding stumbled, and he knew that even the tough mountain horse was nearing the end of its strength. If there was no water in Tonto Creek that would be the end of it . . . they could go no further.

When they had walked what he believed to be a mile, he paused. There was no air stirring below the rim of the hills, and it was stifling. It was, he guessed, more than a hundred and twenty in the shade, if a man could find shade.

The green line marking the creek was nearer now, but he could see no gleam of water among the trees.

His shirt was stiff with caked sweat and dust. He started on, and the horse, after one complaining tug on the reins, followed after.

Taggart was hard put to keep his feet. Heat waves shimmered before him, and at times he had difficulty in bringing his eyes to a focus. He was a big man, unusually quick on his feet, and when he started to stumble he knew he was in trouble. And then he fell.

13

For a long minute he lay sprawled on the ground. Then he got his palms under him and pushed up, getting to his knees, and then to his feet, where he stood swaying. The green line of the creek was weaving weirdly before him.

He had been in trouble before. Swante Taggart could remember few times when he had not been in some kind of trouble. Born in a Conestoga wagon on the Sweetwater in Wyoming, during a wagon-train fight with Cheyennes in 1848, he had lived the following twelve years drifting with his parents from one boom mining camp in California to another. When his father died his mother took him back to the Middle West, and they arrived in Minnesota to live with relatives, just in time for his mother to be massacred by Little Crow's warriors, along with several hundred others.

Young Swante had escaped by hiding under some roots at the edge of a river, and had been found there by Lieutenant Ambrose Freeman when he led his company of Rangers to the relief of Fort Abercrombie. A good hand with a rifle and already a man grown, young Swante rode along.

After the massacre Swante Taggart rode west hunting the Sioux who had killed his mother, for he had seen them all and knew he would remember them. There had been four in that particular group, although there were more outside and around, but it was those four he wanted.

He killed one of them near the edge of a slough not far from Birch Coulee, and two weeks later he found two of the others together near a bend of the Missouri. He killed one and the other got a bullet into Swante and hung around two days while Swante waited in a buffalo wallow.

When a troop of cavalry appeared, the Sioux tried to leave, but Swante's first bullet dropped his horse and the second nailed the Indian as he got up from where he had been thrown when his horse fell. A doctor with the Sibley command fixed Swante up, and he returned to Fort Lincoln in an army ambulance.

In the years that followed he herded cattle, hunted buffalo, scouted for the Army, and rode shotgun on a stage. While he was holding down this last job, a party

14

of Sioux approached the stage north of Hat Creek Station in Wyoming, and one of them was the last of the four who had killed his mother. They knew each other, and Swante told the others what he wanted. While the stage waited, Swante fought the warrior with a knife and killed him, and then got back up on the box and the stage rolled on to Deadwood.

In New Mexico he found a spring with a good flow and two meadows that lay below it. He filed on the land and settled down to fight Apaches and live happily ever after. The Apaches gave him no trouble, but after almost a year of peaceful living the Bennett brothers drove six thousand head of cattle into the area and found the range they wanted . . . only Swante Taggart sat right in the middle of it by the biggest spring, and with several hundred acres of sub-irrigated land. The three Bennetts and their gun-fighting *segundo* rode over to suggest that Swante move, but Swante was not accepting suggestions.

Threats followed and Swante sat tight. He owned two hundred head of cattle and a few horses, and he was contented. He asked only to be left alone.

Then there had been a "difficulty." Young Jim Bennett decided the time to act was now, and with Rusty Bob Blazer, who had killed three men in Texas, he rode over to move Taggart.

The shooting was sudden, offhand, and Jim Bennett and Rusty Bob lay dying on the grass, and the only witnesses were Bennett riders.

It was a bad time for gun trouble. New Mexico was in a ferment over the activities of young Billy Bonney, who was rousting around in the middle of a shooting war up in Lincoln County. The Bennett brothers had money, cattle, and strong political influence, while Swante Taggart had only a fast horse.

A man must use what he has.

Outlawed by the state for what had been a justifiable killing, Swante Taggart and his fast horse headed west. A pack horse carried what supplies were at hand when the dream ended.

The stop at Knight's Ranch had been his mistake. Until that time he had avoided trails, but by the time he rode within sight of Knight's he was out of coffee, out of food, and he desperately needed sleep. Until then nobody had any idea what had become of Taggart.

Two days later when Pete Shoyer came in, returning from delivering a body to the sheriff in Silver City, he heard Taggart was wanted and discovered a man of the description had been at Knight's.

Crown King had seemed the obvious solution for Taggart. It was a mine, a scattering of other prospect holes, and a few buildings. Scarcely a town, it was off the main trail and offered a job for a man who could use a single-jack and drill. Taggart had learned how to do that in California when he was ten, and he was doing all right until Pete Shoyer rode into town.

Within minutes, while Shoyer was cutting the dust from his throat in the Crown King saloon, Swante Taggart rode out. He went up Poland Canyon, switched back down Horsethief Canyon, rode through the Bradshaw Mountains, and watered his horse in the cold waters of Agua Fria opposite Squaw Creek Mesa.

Half a dozen canyons open in the raw side of Squaw Creek Mesa, each seeming to offer a means of escape, but actually the only trail led up the wall and not through the inviting canyons. He believed he had an hour's lead and he might have more, and what hoof-prints the horse might leave in the clear stream bottom would be gone by that time, so Swante Taggart had ridden upstream for two miles and left the water on a ledge of rock. He camped that night close to Shirt-Tail Springs, with Turret Peak looming to the northwest.

It was here only a few years earlier that Major Randall's soldiers had scaled the fortress-like peak in the night to surprise a band of Apaches in their seemingly invulnerable hiding place.

That had been several days ago, and now he was here, weaving heavily down the long slope toward Tonto Creek with the heat waves dancing weirdly before him, with cracked lips, a parched throat, and a prayer for water in the Creek. His head ached, throbbing heavily, and the sun blazed in the brassy vault of the sky. The ground was hot beneath his boots.

16

The Apache came out of the ground as if born from it, and he came shooting, but even an Apache can be wrong. The mistake killed him.

The dust-brown figure leaped, the sunlight caught on his rifle barrel, and Swante Taggart, who had used a fast draw before this, felt the gun buck in his hard palm.

The mountains tossed the sound like a bouncing ball. Then the sound faded and died, and Swante Taggart stood staring at a dead Indian and knew he had been lucky. There had been no time for thought . . . his reaction had been instantaneous, the result of years of practice and awareness of danger.

The Apache pony hated the white man's smell and drew back from him. There was no water skin on the pony, and Taggart took time only to secure the rifle and ammunition. There was thirty-odd rounds of .44 ammunition, and before this was over he might need it. Staggering a little as he straightened up, Swante Taggart glanced around him.

How long since the others had gone by? He had come three miles . . . nearly four, and they must have gone as far or farther. He gathered the gelding's reins and started on once more, plodding along, his eyes staring into the heat-blurred mystery into which he walked.

And then green leaves were brushing his face and with a grunt of longing he burst through the brush into the bed of the Tonto.

It was dry.

Three times before, some years earlier, Swante Taggart had camped beside Tonto Creek or watered his horse there, but now, when he needed it so much there was no water in it.

It was twenty miles to Turkey Spring, and through a mind fogged by exhaustion he knew he was not going to make it. Nor was his horse.

The slight breeze from the south brought no reaction from the steeldust, and had there been water in a pool of the stream bed to the south, Swante knew the horse would have smelled it. If water there was, anywhere near, it must lie to the north. Turning, he plodded along the sandy bed, each step a special effort of will.

And then he fell again.

He did not stumble this time. He seemed to be wading in sand, and each step seemed to take him deeper and deeper, until he fell face down in the sand.

For several minutes he lay prone until the nudging of the gelding stirred him to action. Slowly, he got to his feet.

A faint sound came to him, and he turned his head like a man in sleep, struggling to place the sound. A cottonwood . . . leaves rustling. The whispering leaves spoke of water. And then that sound again, a scratching and rustling. Carefully, he worked his way into the brush on the stream's bank, but exhaustion had robbed him of guile and he made the brush rustle. Instantly, the sound he had been moving toward stopped.

After a moment of silence it began once more. Pushing his way through the brush, he emerged a dozen feet from the base of a giant cottonwood. Nearby two porcupines were digging for water.

The hole they had dug was only as large as a good-sized water bucket but the last of the sand was damp.

He picked up a rock and shied it at them, but they stood their ground, quills bristling. Swante Taggart moved toward them and reluctantly they backed off, giving ground slowly.

The gelding had followed him and it went to the hole, sniffing eagerly at the damp sand, and scratching at it with one hoof.

Pulling the horse away, Swante knelt and began to scoop sand from the hole with both hands. The sand became damper, and he was down less than two feet. He dug on, working feverishly, and soon the hole began to fill with muddy water.

Swante sank back on his heels, and let the steeldust have the first of the water. Then pushing the horse away, he dug the hole deeper, widened it out. The porcupines had not left him. They waited on the edge of the brush making angry sounds at him, their need for water overcoming their fear of him.

He would make it then . . . he would drink and the horse would drink and he would fill the canteen. Then he would leave the water to the porcupines, and they deserved it. He dipped his cupped hands into the water and gulped a mouthful which he held in his mouth, letting

18

the parched tissues soak it up ever so gradually, then allowing a cool trickle to find its way down his raw throat.

The gelding whinnied pleadingly and he allowed the horse to drink again, although there was scarcely more than a swallow or two in the bottom of the hole. He scooped out more sand and the hole began to fill up. He managed another swallow, and a delicious coolness began to spread through him.

There was shade under the cottonwood, and conceal-ment, so he stretched out on the sand and lay still, relax-ing little by little as exhaustion took over. From time to time the horse drank, then he began cropping on some brown grass nearby. Swante lay still and listened to the sounds, and he heard the porcupines sucking at the water.

Turning his head he saw them there, watching him warily, but drinking, too, not six feet from where he lay.

When they were gone he cleaned out the pool and dug into his pack for what remained of his coffee. He built a small fire of dry sticks under the cottonwood and made the coffee. Desperately as he wanted food, he would not kill one of the porcupines, for they had brought him to water. Actually they had saved his life.

No desert man will camp near a water-hole, for water in the desert is too precious to others beside himself, and wild creatures will not approach a water-hole when a man is near. The porcupines had been a rare exception, their need perhaps as great as his own.

When he left the water-hole, it was only to move back a short distance, for he needed time to recover from the effects of his long thrist. He spread his blanket and slept, too soundly for safety, but with the sleep of utter exhaus-tion.

He awakened before daylight and led the gelding to the hole, where they both drank again, and when fresh water, now clear and cold, had collected again, he filled his canteen. The porcupines had been there during the night, for the marks of their tiny hands were all about.

The sun was just showing itself over the mountains when he finally left. The place where he had found water was in the mouth of a wash running into Tonto Creek from the Sierra Anchas; and emerging from the brush, he found a faint Indian trail that led back into the mountains, running alongside the wash. There were no signs of recent travel.

It was not the trail he had been planning to take, but it was one even less likely to be discovered. Without doubt it led to the top of the plateau.

Following this trail into a notch in the Sierra Anchas, he drew up in the shade of a massive cliff, and turning in the saddle he glanced back along the way he had come.

Wind moved stealthily among the piñons on the mountain near him, breathing cool and fragrant across his heat-baked cheeks, and behind him the land lay vast and empty under the blazing sun. The Tonto Creek valley, the Mazatal Mountains riding beyond it.

Nothing . . .

The land lay vast, red-brown-pink. Sand-colored mountains splashed with the green of juniper. Here and there were shadows of clouds, and occasional shadows in the lee of cliffs, but otherwise it was a red-brown-pink monotony.

Something . . . there was something. Very distant, very faint, there was dust. A stirring of dust that was not a dust-devil, but someone, somebody coming.

So they were still behind him. They were still coming.

Chapter 3

The sky was faintly gray when Miriam Stark climbed the thread of trail to the top of Rockinstraw Mountain, a single rose-tinted cloud above the horizon giving only a suggestion of the glory to come with sunrise. Yet there was enough light to see the web of faint trails, each leading to some vantage point from which the country could be observed.

She loved this place, for even on the hottest day there was a faint stirring of wind, and always there was silence, an unbelievable silence that left the mind free to wander without interruption.

Taking her station behind a juniper, Miriam began the

methodical search of the terrain, using the system taught her by Adam. First a quick, sharp survey of the area closest to the mountain, in case somebody had approached during the darker hours, and then the eyes lifted to the farthest horizon and searched with infinite care every canyon, every possible route, every place where men might camp or hide.

She knew what to look for. Any movement, any change in the pattern of shadows, any flickering, any alteration of any kind at all in the familiar terrain. She had learned to distinguish smoke from dust, and to tell after a brief glance whether dust was caused by a dust-devil, a flurry of wind, or the passage of mounted men . . . or man.

This study of the terrain, this careful search for any traveler, this continual awareness was not a matter of diversion, but was a matter of life and death. They existed here in a precarious situation, and a careless movement, a careless track, or a chance sighting by some Apache or drifting white man could mean the end of everything; it could even mean death.

Twice each day one or the other of them came to this place and studied the country around. As there were only three of them, there was no way they could continually keep one person on lookout, and the study of the country at dawn and sunset represented the closest alternative.

Rough as the country was, by now they knew it well. Due south and north were the areas of greatest danger. There were canyons and arroyos and considerable cover, but long ago, when they first arrived, each of them had ridden these canyons, studied them, and knew where the cover was to be found.

On the west the only danger lay in the openings between the mesas, for no one would come across the tops. On this side the descent was gradual, but on the far side they fell steeply away to Pinal Creek.

This morning, after a brief survey, Miriam directed all her attention to the north. Two creeks entered the Salt River from the north in this vicinity—Coon Creek and Cherry Creek. Her view up the basin of each was nearly perfect, but only a tenderfoot would chance coming along such a route.

Red arrows shot sunlight into the heavens, and the

21

ridges to the east were crowned with gold and rose. Crushing some cedar foliage in her hands, she sniffed their aromatic smell. Nowhere in all that vast expanse did anything move . . . the air was astonishingly clear, and from where she stood she could see miles upon miles.

When first she saw the speck she did not believe it was a man . . . yet intuitively she knew it must be. A moment before the speck had not been there, and then it was, and now . . . it was gone!

Only for an instant had something been visible there, some moving thing upon the bare slope of Black Mesa, just beyond Salt River. There had only been the one speck, so if it was a man it seemed almost certain that it was a white man.

Curious and puzzled, she directed her glass toward the area and inspected it with care, but it was beyond the practical range of the glass and she detected nothing more. Yet something had been there, and now it was gone.

If it had been a man he had chosen a way never traveled, but one that would allow him a good view of his back trail and the surrounding country. From below he would not be visible, and it was unlikely anybody would be above him, for due to the conformation of the mesa, going higher would be pure waste of time.

She left her position and worked her way around the top of the mountain, studying the country in every direction. Their lives depended on remaining unknown to the Apaches who occasionally passed through, and so far they had been secure.

Adam came up the mountain and met her at the first position. "See anything?"

"A rider, I think." She indicated the bare spot on the shoulder of Black Mesa. "Can he get down to the river from there?"

Adam took the glasses and studied the place. "I killed a deer over there the first week we were here. Yes, he can come down, all right."

He studied the area again. "No sign of anyone now."

"There won't be. I have a feeling he doesn't wish to be seen."

He made a slow search of the country. "Connie doesn't

22

like it here," he commented suddenly. "I don't blame her, exactly."

"She's had enough, I think," Miriam responded. "She had it before we did, you know. She grew up with it."

"Is she afraid?"

Miriam considered the question. "Aren't we all? I think she is less afraid than we are. She's a strong woman."

"I know . . . and she believes I'm weak."

"You love her, don't you?"

"As I never loved anyone." He lowered the glasses. "There *is* somebody over there." He handed her the glasses. "See? On the cliff above the river?"

"I see him. He's looking for a way down."

They were silent as Adam took back the glasses and watched the far-off figure.

"Yes, I love her," he said after a moment. "I loved her from the first day we met, and I believed she would come to love me."

"I think she does." As she spoke, Miriam was surprised to realize she really believed it. "I don't believe she knows that she loves you, or how much, but she doesn't believe you are strong."

"I know."

"He's found a way," Miriam said, watching through the glasses. "He's coming down."

Adam took the glasses when she offered them and studied the distant figure of the man on horseback. "One man alone in this country . . . it doesn't look right."

"He could be an outlaw."

Adam continued to watch the rider. "When we've gold enough we'll go out," he said. "I know the ranch I want, and once I have it we can go to San Francisco or even back east. After that I think Connie will feel different . . . and I'm planning a real house, something she can be proud of."

He passed the glasses to his sister. "He's across . . . he's disappeared in the brush on this side."

He caught her shoulder. "Look! West of him . . . see the dust?"

She shifted the glasses to study the dust cloud, and saw a war party of perhaps a dozen Apaches, traveling in the same direction as the strange rider, but some distance from him.

There was no way they could warn him without revealing their position. And Consuelo was alone at the house.

"Apaches," she said.

He got to his feet. "Let's get back before they cut us off."

They snatched their rifles and almost ran down the steep trail. At the canyon they could defend themselves, but caught out like this they would be killed in a matter of minutes if they were seen, and alone in the canyon Consuelo could do little. The lone rider must shift for himself.

Swante Taggart rode down off the mesa and into the water. At this point it was scarcely knee-deep for the horse, and a few minutes later Swante rode up the bank and into the willows along the river.

Dismounting there under cover of the brush, he trailed his reins and walked back to the edge of the water. With a clump of sage he brushed out his tracks and sifted dry sand over them until all evidence of his crossing had been eliminated. On the other side of the river he had been riding across shelving rock.

He worked his way through the brush, leading his horse, and paused in the outer edge and with his field glasses studied the mountains ahead of him. Only a few minutes earlier Adam and Miriam Stark had fled down the trail, but he was too late to have seen them there, and their route led down a deep, water-worn cut.

Still leading the steeldust, he went up an arroyo. Suddenly he felt the horse's head come up and saw his ears prick. "Easy, boy!" he whispered. "Easy, now."

The gelding turned slightly toward him, but the ears remained pricked, listening. And then Swante Taggart heard the sound himself, a click of a hoof on stone.

Drawing the horse back under the slight overhang, he waited, rifle in hand.

The shadow of a riding Indian appeared on the far wall, then another, then several. One hand on the nose of the steeldust, Swante waited, his heart pounding heavily. Sweat trickled down his cheeks, and inside he was cold and still. A pebble fell near him, then a trickle of sand. Letting go the gelding's nose, he lifted his rifle.

He could hear the low mutter of their voices, for they were scarcely fifteen feet above him. They argued briefly, and then moved off along the edge of the arroyo, and he knew enough of their language to know they were looking for something. But what? *Who?*

He squatted on his heels against the wall, the rifle across his knees. It was growing hot.

His canteen was full, but he knew that neither the horse nor himself could go on as they had . . . they must find a place and hole up for a rest. Also, Shoyer must still be on the trail, and the reason was obvious, for there were only two places he might be going . . . to Globe or to Morenci.

The thing to do was to stop. If a man left no tracks none could be found, and Pete Shoyer would go on to Globe, then to Morenci, looking for him.

It was a risky thing to try, and he would need food, which meant either trapping or shooting game, and shooting was likely to attract Apaches. He must find a place with water for himself and grass for the gelding.

When half an hour had gone by he rolled and lighted a cigarette to still the gnawing of hunger. Hunger, however, was not new to him, and he was not a man who pampered himself.

When a full hour had passed he climbed to the rim of the arroyo and sat among the rocks to study the country. There should be springs somewhere around the mountain to the east, which was Rockinstraw, for run-off water had a way of coming to the surface. Any spring would be a danger, for the Apaches were almost sure to know of it and visit it from time to time.

As he started to rise, a rabbit jumped up and he seized a rock . . . the rabbit was gone. Probably couldn't have hit it, anyway. He had never been much good at throwing things . . . except lead once in a while.

The Apaches had gone off to the south. His own way led to the east, so he mounted and started on.

Desert though it was, the country was brushy. There was prickly pear, pin oak, and a variety of desert growth, so that a man riding slowly to raise no dust, and taking advantage of the brush and juniper, could keep under cover at least half the time.

With Rockinstraw Mountain looming ahead of him, he worked his way slowly across country, stopping frequently, constantly aware of danger from Apaches, but equally ready to observe the slight touch of green that might mean a spring or small seep.

Ahead of him in a canyon bottom was a heavy stand of brush, and pushing up to it, he noticed that some of the brush was dead. He paused, studying the situation. What it was that first arrested his attention he did not know, and anyone riding less cautiously than he would have noticed nothing, but something about the area disturbed him.

The patch of thick brush lay in the shallow opening of the canyon, and Taggart skirted the brush warily, trying to decide what it was that bothered him. Dismounting, he walked into the brush leading his horse. Glancing from time to time at the steeldust, he noticed nothing. If there was anything alive around, the horse was as unaware of it as he himself.

His eye caught the abrasion before his attention came to a focus on it. He had taken a step past when he suddenly became aware of what he had seen, and turning back he looked again.

The trunk of a twisted mesquite tree had been bruised by some heavy object. Nor was the bruise in such a place that it might have been caused by a horse's hoof . . . the abrasion was higher, but not fresh. He studied it, knowing that his life now hung precariously and any slight mistake could mean its end.

Squatting, he turned his head and looked around, and so it was that he saw the wheel.

It was a wagon wheel, almost entirely concealed in brush, but beyond it there was another wheel. Ducking under the brush, crawling on his knees, he reached the wagon.

A wagon concealed in such a manner meant that whoever concealed it meant to find it again, but intended that it should not be found by anyone else. How anybody had gotten a wagon this far was more than he could conceive, yet the wagon was here.

The presence of a wagon must mean the presence of men. He studied the bottom of the wagon as much as he could in the concealing brush. There were some threads that must have come from burlap sacking . . . and caught on a sliver of the wagon-board was a cotton thread. He scowled . . . from a woman's skirt? It seemed ridiculous, and yet . . .

The tracks had been wiped out, but not by one skilled in tracking. Searching, he found a partial hoof-print under the edge of a bush . . . the wagon had been drawn by mules.

Returning to the steeldust, he lighted another smoke and considered the situation. Whoever had brought the wagon this far could have taken it farther; hence it was logical to suppose that the driver had reached his destination, or close to it.

Had the wagon been abandoned because his animals had been killed, at least a skeleton would have remained.

What would a man be doing in this country? Cattle were impractical with the Apaches on the loose, although here and there a few were trying it. But he had seen no cattle, nor any signs of them.

Mining?

That might explain the wagon, brought in to carry supplies and equipment. Why not bring it in on mules? Or horses? But if the man did have a woman along, he might prefer a wagon, or if he were bringing a large amount of supplies, planning a long stay.

For one man alone or even a half-dozen men to remain in this country during Apache trouble meant a secure position, well-fortified, well-supplied.

Of course, it was always possible the wagon had been so cumbersome they had decided to abandon it, but then the wagon would most likely have been left in the open, wherever the driver had stopped. There was no reason to conceal the wagon unless the owner was expecting to remain nearby, and expecting to use it again.

The dryness of the cut brush indicated that the wagon had been left there something around a month ago, and if the driver of that wagon was not dead, he must be somewhere within a radius of three or four miles, and the chances were it would be less.

Where one man stopped another could. That man would need water, grass, a place of hiding or defense. It would be a place, more than likely, where a man could hole up for a while.

While the steeldust cropped at the mesquite brush, Swante Taggart continued to study the situation, remembering the terrain he had examined so carefully. He had expected there would be springs near Rockinstraw, and it must be near one of these that the man had located.

At present Taggart was hidden from observation and his horse was contented with the brush. Taking his rifle, canteen, and field glasses, he found a way to the top of the bank and lay down among the rocks and brush.

It was very hot . . . no sound disturbed the clear air. The smells of hot, dry grass and mesquite came to him. Shielding the field glasses with his sombrero so they would not reflect sunlight, he began a careful study of the country ahead of him. But after some time he had found nothing—no clue, no sign of anything, any object that did not belong, no evidence of a trail anywhere, nothing to indicate the presence of human beings.

Returning to the brush, he loosened the saddle girth and picketed the gelding. Then he stretched out in the shade and slept.

No more than an hour had passed when he opened his eyes. Near him the horse dozed. He got to his feet and, taking the glasses, went back to his former position and began a new study of the country, realizing that a change in the position of the sun would often change the looks of an area in a decided manner.

He should search, but he did not like the idea of leaving tracks around that might be seen by either Apaches or Pete Shoyer.

More and more his attention was drawn back to Rockinstraw. The mountain loomed above everything in a country that was almighty broken up. From its peak a man could get quite a view, but he could also get himself shot at.

By now it was late afternoon. Within an hour or two, if anyone was around they would be preparing something to eat, and that meant a fire, and a fire meant smoke.

Very little smoke if the fellow used dry wood, but smoke just the same. And smoke could be smelled and seen.

Swante Taggart rolled a cigarette and lit up. He would wait . . . he was sure he was right. Somebody was hidden close by, and a hiding place that good would be good for him also.

He would wait.

Chapter 4

The Spanish fathers who had located the canyon of the lost mine had mistaken float for an outcropping, and without doubt there had been a lot of the float, and some large boulders included. Few of the padres had any knowledge of mining or of the occurrence of ores, and what they found had apparently been broken off from high up on the mountain, from which point it had rolled or floated down and wedged among other rocks. Later, though realizing their mistake, they had failed to discover the true source of the gold.

Adam Stark knew they had failed because he found evidence of their efforts and their failure, but he had been more fortunate because he had known considerably more about mining geology.

Whether the padres had given up and returned to Mexico or had been murdered by Apaches he had no idea, although he suspected the former. Certainly, there was no evidence of any battle at the canyon of the chapel. There were no skulls, no human bones of any kind, and no weapons lying about. If they had been killed it would have been after leaving this place. At no time had he found any Indian remains in the canyon itself.

Considering his own situation, Adam Stark knew that two months at the present rate would leave him with more than a hundred thousand in free gold, all sacked up and ready to take out . . . if they lasted that long.

Neither Consuelo or Miriam had ever seen the source

of the gold, and he had no intention that they should. His excuse had been accepted without discussion or apparent curiosity: the fewer tracks in the vicinity, the better.

The truth was that every instant he worked at the vein his life was in danger, and not from Apaches, but from the nature of the rock itself. He was undermining the base of a leaning tower of rock that might at any time come down, burying him beneath a heap of rubble.

The ever-present risk of discovery by Apaches or by white outlaws occupied the minds of the two women until all else seemed relatively unimportant. But they lived a day-to-day existence, never allowing these dangers to become a settled fear.

Neither of them considered the problem of the mining itself. To their few questions Adam had been casual in comment. "It's slow work," he said, "mainly hacking it out of the native rock and getting it down the mountain."

He had left it at that, and so had they. The actual fact of the matter was something quite different.

In his quest for the gold, Adam Stark had followed the alluvial fan up the side of the mountain. The fan was merely a cascade of rocky debris tumbled down the steep slope as a result of thousands of years of weathering on the heights above.

Struggling upward, compelled to use his hands in places because of the steepness of the slope, he had come at last to the source of the gold in a band of rotten quartz all of six feet wide and cobwebbed with gold.

At a glance he knew the discovery was almost unbelievable, and if it was from broken-off bits of this rock that the padres had taken their gold, he could appreciate what excitement they must have felt.

Yet even in his moment of success some warning in the beetling brow of cliff kept him from going forward. His innate caution gripped him, and he drew back a little to examine the situation more carefully. Wary of what he saw, he circled the granitic upthrust and then climbed to the ridge behind it where he could look down upon the roof. What he saw left him dry-mouthed and jittery.

Obviously the upthrust was part of a much older range, one long weathered and worn, suffering from shock and twisting, until finally this tower of rock had been violently upthrust to leave it standing a shaky ruin among younger and sturdier peaks. In the processes of the past the rock had been shattered and riven by mighty forces until it had become a miner's nightmare.

With enormous wealth here for the taking, every single ounce must be taken at the risk of death. One stick of powder might bring the whole crumbling mass down in a heap, and it towered three hundred feet or more above its base. The roof of the mass was riven with cracks, seamed with breaks like the wall of an ancient building left standing after heavy shelling.

Walking back to the vein, Adam Stark found he could actually break off pieces with his fingers, and this vein itself lay on the downhill side and at the very base of the tower of rock. The upthrust leaned at such an angle that a man working at the vein would be cutting his way into the very foundation of the tower, and a single blow might bring the whole mass down upon him.

Furthermore, if the towering mass should fall, even if he were not under it, the vein would be hopelessly buried under thousands of tons of rock and beyond his power to recover.

Adam Stark had backed off from the pinnacle and, seating himself on a rock, had lighted his pipe. A man might, he reflected, take tons out of there without it collapsing upon him . . . or it might come down with the first blow. Yet he knew that, wanting that gold as he did, he had no choice.

In his own mind he was sure Connie loved him as he did her, and he believed that once she had her chance to see something of the world outside, she would return to what she knew, content to settle down. She was, after all, a Mexican woman, and a Mexican woman without a husband is nobody among her people. She becomes an object of sympathy from some and contempt from others, and is nothing to herself. If she does not have a husband she has failed in woman's main objective. He knew that Consuelo believed that, and believed it deeply, but hers had been a life of struggle since the beginning, and what she wanted was her moment of glamor.

Maybe he was a fool, but he knew that without Consuelo nothing made sense, and he wished her to have what she wanted, and he wanted also the pleasure of giving. All of that depended on the gold that lay before him.

Studying the tower of rock, he knew he had already accepted its challenge. He was going after the gold.

But even as he made his decision, he knew that there were two things he must guard against. The first was tolerance of danger that might bring carelessness, and the second was going back for that little bit more that would kill him.

He would have to make his decision now, and stay with that decision. He must decide on how much he wanted and take no more, but he must always be prepared to quit with less if the situation demanded.

He wanted a hundred thousand dollars.

It seemed a lot. When he had started this trip he would have been content with ten thousand, and until a few minutes ago he would have settled for that much. Now he was already in danger because his demands had risen in accordance with the amount of gold in sight.

There must be nearly a thousand dollars lying in rocky debris upon the slope right under the tower, a thousand dollars just for the picking up.

He would take that first. He would gather it, sack it up, take it down to the canyon, and get out the gold. Then if anything happened to him, his wife and sister would still have enough money to take them to wherever they wished to live.

Even then, having made his decision, he did not go forward, but sat there and refilled his pipe. The chances were that if the tower collapsed he would be caught beneath it, unless he could get a running start. No man could run in the soft gravel of the upper slope, so he would take slabs of rock and build a walk. Then, if he had a chance to run he would not be bogged down in sand.

He must be deliberate in all his actions, and he must never forget for an instant the towering mass that loomed above him; for a split second of hesitation would mean death and burial under tons of rock.

Rising, he knocked out his pipe and gathered together a sack of the loose ore, all of it larded with gold. When the sack was filled with as much as he could carry, he put it on his shoulder and started down the mountain by an easier route his eyes picked out on the slope.

The padres had used an *arrastra* to break up the rock and get out the gold, but he dared take no such risk. The rumble of an *arrastra* could be heard for some distance, and he had no desire to attract attention. The blows of a hammer were more easily muffled, although the process was slower.

Returning to the canyon of the chapel, Adam considered his plans. The mining town of Globe was but a short distance to the south but he had never visited the town and did not plan to. His visit would arouse discussion and might lead someone to follow him back out of curiosity. They had brought with them a good supply of beans, rice, flour, and dried fruit, besides other staples, and this, augmented by what game he could trap and the edible plants Consuelo knew so well, would have to suffice.

The opening of the small canyon, partly concealed by desert growth, presented an uninteresting aspect that promised nothing to a rider passing by. Any desert traveler has passed hundreds of such arroyos or canyons with scarcely a passing glance. It was in a small cove at the upper end of the canyon that they pastured their horses and mules.

Consuelo stepped from the door when Miriam and Adam came down from the mountain. She held a rifle in her hand. "Somebody comes?" she asked.

"Apaches," Miriam said. "And a white man."

Consuelo laughed. "It is Tom Sanifer. He comes for me, just like he said."

"Then he'd better watch his hair," Adam replied dryly. "He's in a fair way to lose it."

"He will come. You see. Tom Sanifer loves me."

Adam placed his rifle beside the door and dipped a gourd dipper into the wooden bucket beside the door. He looked across it at his wife. "And you'd go?"

She returned his look mockingly. "Who knows? Maybe you keel him. Maybe he keel you, and then I must go with him."

"I think you'll stay," Adam said quietly.

"Here?" Her temper flared. "You think I like this place? You think this is good place for woman? Just give me one chance and I go . . . *queeck!*"

She took her rifle and walked to the mouth of the canyon to keep watch while Miriam and Adam ate. When Adam had finished he lighted his pipe and, taking his rifle, went out to relieve Consuelo.

She came back, and began the work of cleaning up while Miriam went on with her meal. As she ate, she read from one of their carefully hoarded books.

Consuelo stared at her. "Always you read . . . you no want a man, you want a book. You want even to sleep with a book!"

"It might be better than some men," Miriam replied dryly. "And you don't have to wash socks for a book."

When she had finished eating she walked to the end of the canyon. Adam stepped down from the rocks. "I believe they've gone on," he said, "but we can't be sure."

She went up among the rocks and found her place—a place that allowed her to hear anyone approaching, yet her own shadow was lost against the blacker shadow of the rocks.

Night had come while she ate. Darkness lay now like velvet upon the land, and overhead the sky was midnight blue and scattered with stars, with only an occasional cloud. She knew the desert night, knew the amazing clarity of it, and all the little sounds the desert had that belonged to it, and she loved these hours beneath the stars.

They rarely stood watch, and that only when someone had been seen in the vicinity, and on those occasions they often stood guard most of the night. On one occasion they stood watch for three days and nights.

When Stark went back and entered the house, Consuelo turned to face him. "When we go, Adam? How much longer do we 'ave to stay here?"

"Two months . . . a little less or a little more."

"You know what I think? I think we never go. I think we die here in this canyon. I think so."

"The gold is richer now."

She ignored the comment. "You know what Apache do to man they catch? I have seen it. They tie him to a cactus with strips of green rawhide, and when it dries it tightens and pulls the thorns into a man. He dies . . . after a long time and much pain."

"You saw *that?*"

"I saw . . . and what they do to a woman I have seen. Before I was six, I have seen it."

"I never saw anything like that. Hope I never do."

Consuelo put a glass on a shelf. "Why Miriam no marry? She afraid?"

"Miriam?" Adam chuckled. "I don't think the devil himself could frighten Miriam. No, she just knows the kind of man she wants and she isn't going to settle for less, no matter how long she has to wait."

"I think she is fool."

"We're all fools after a fashion. Look at me . . . I gave up a law practice because I wanted a ranch of my own, I wanted to be in the cattle business. So I studied geology and came west to find the gold to buy the ranch. . . like a lot of other dreamers."

"I think you fool." She paused. "Adam, we are no good for each other. Once I think I love you, but I was wrong."

"Maybe you expect too much of me, Connie. Or maybe you're looking for the wrong things in a marriage."

She stared gloomily from the window. "Maybe I am bad. Maybe I am meant for bad girl. You are good man but you are frighten, Adam. You are frighten of Tom Sanifer."

There was no anger in Adam. "He must have impressed you, Connie. That's why I worry about you, because you're impressed by the wrong things."

He leaned back in his chair. "Tom Sanifer was a fine-looking man, but he was an empty man. I'm afraid you mistake the appearance of strength for strength itself."

"The first chance I get, I leave you, Adam. I am finish. You don't say I don't tell you. And you have no right to speak of Tom Sanifer. He told you he would come back for me, and he told you he would kill you."

"It is a small man who talks big before women. If you must leave me, let it be for a really good man, not an empty bucket like Tom Sanifer."

Miriam stood in the desert silence, listening for sounds

she hoped not to hear, sounds long practice had taught her to distinguish from the usual night sounds of the desert.

She was very still among the rocks, absorbing the cool beauty of the desert night. At the canyon's mouth the sky's breadth was enormous, vastly greater than in the narrow canyon. In the north the Big Dipper hung in the sky among its legion of accompanying stars. The dark outline of Rockinstraw Mountain shouldered against the sky, part of its top curiously flattened, looking like a turret, or perhaps a pulpit.

There is no other night that has the stillness and the beauty of the desert night . . . the sea when it is quiet comes closest to that stillness that is not stillness, but the sea is always alive. The Arctic, too, has its own beauty, but the desert is still with a curious alert stillness, a sense of listening, of poised awareness. Standing alone in the desert at night one feels that all about one there is this listening, an alertness for movement, for life, for change.

The weirdly shaped figures of stone, eroded by years, the serrated ridges, the white stillness of the *playas* and the challenging fingers of the sahuaro . . . these are there, or the clustered canes of the ocotillo. The desert is always, by day or night, but especially by night, a place of mystery.

Standing against the rocks, Miriam looked out over the desert, and against the sky overhead she saw the swoop of a bat. After minutes she heard a rush of wings that might have been an owl. Sand trickled . . . something rustled in the sand nearby . . . all else was quiet.

And then she heard another sound, a faint stir of movement not far off, a sound that was not of the night, and not of the desert. She knew the sound because she had heard it many times before when she herself rode in the desert . . . it was the brush of cedar against a saddle . . . a rustle of sound she recognized at once.

The mysterious rider came up out of the lower draw and was for a moment or two outlined sharply against the night sky, and then the horse walked into the open not far from her.

Poised . . . half-frightened, she waited, fearing to move because he might hear the slightest sound, but aware of something in the approaching figure that warned her of an equal awareness in him.

The rider came toward her and then turned slightly to the right and stopped, not fifty feet away from her. From where she stood he was partially in silhouette, a big, fine figure of a man on a splendidly built horse.

She knew she was invisible to him, for more than once she had stood where he stood and had been unable to see Adam standing where she now stood. Yet the rider had stopped.

Did he guess her presence? How could he? He had seemed to be searching for something, coming on slowly as he had, and there was no trail he could be following here unless it was some intangible trail, some sense of things in the night that drew him on.

It could not have been smoke from the evening fire, for that would be out now . . . unless some lingering aroma of it still hung in the air. The canyon had a way of drawing smoke back up along its length and up the flank of the mountain, and none of them had ever detected smoke in this place.

Yet the rider made no move to ride on. She heard the faintest rustle of paper and knew he was rolling a smoke. She heard a match strike, and caught only a brief glimpse of a strongly cut face in the brief flare of the match cupped in his hands. He drew deep on the cigarette and she saw the end glow like a firefly in the night.

Who was he? What was he? Why had he stopped at this place?

He was without doubt the rider they had seen earlier when he crossed the Salt River north of them, but where had he been in the meantime, and why was he here?

She dared not move, for she knew he would hear the slightest sound. Nor did she wish to leave, for there was some intangible awareness of each other that held her still, breathless and waiting in the night.

She saw him remove his hat and run his fingers through his hair. His horse stamped impatiently, eager to be moving, and when he shifted his weight in the saddle, the leather creaked. Suddenly she felt a wild desire to speak out, to question him, to find who he was and where he was going, but most of all, why he had stopped here.

Yet she was hesitant to speak or to move for fear that the slightest sound or movement would shatter the moment's spell and leave her with nothing. As long as they both were silent, the intangible communion between them existed, and he remained for her the stuff of dreams.

In the darkness, unknown as he was, she could clothe him with what personality she would. He could be anyone . . . the lover she had so long desired, the unknown rider that she had known would come sometime, the man who would see her for what she was, who would know her, and want her for his own.

In reality, he might be an outlaw, a thief, a murderer. He might be a renegade white man living among Apaches; and if he was any of these things, to disclose her presence here would be to place herself in jeopardy, and not only herself but Consuelo and Adam.

Yet in the night's vast quiet there was between them this invisible link, forged by some mysterious bond of stars and stillness. They were drawn together by the silence, the loom of mountains, and the deep shadows where the cliffs stood tall. Was he feeling what she felt? Was he, too, sensing that this moment was the stuff of dreams? That here, for the moment at least, each belonged to the other?

She put her hand to her hair in the darkness, feeling suddenly untidy. She had not prepared herself to meet a lover this night, even one who would in a moment touch his horse with a heel and ride on, moving out of her life and away from her consciousness, like all those other faceless, featureless men of whom she had dreamed in the past.

He was there, close to her, a tall, still figure sitting his saddle, and a man who might be . . . anyone.

He might ride on . . . Suddenly, desperately, she wished to say something, some magic word, some phrase that would make him stay, that would draw him to her and keep him close. She knew suddenly that he must not ride on . . . it was here he belonged, beside her.

It was fantastic. The desert night had taken her good sense . . . was she a silly, romantic girl to be lured by shadows?

She was.

The dream gives its magic until the dream is realized, but even then something of the dream remains . . . the aura, the nostalgic, half-realized longing, that stays. And this silent rider, dark upon his horse, until a word was spoken he was hers, and hers alone.

Moments passed, and she was motionless, and the rider sat his saddle. She saw him replace his hat and her throat tightened at the thought that he might now ride on, that replacing the hat was preliminary to a touch of the heel. His cigarette glowed briefly again like a campfire's spark arrested in flight.

"A night like this is like no other night. There is a beauty in it that is scarcely real."

It was a moment before Miriam realized the rider had spoken, and she was startled . . . for in this brief standing still of time he had become almost a creation of her fantasy.

"It is the desert."

There was a silence then that neither broke for minutes. Then he said, "It is late for you to be out."

It was something that might have been said to a young girl in New England, in some village there, after midnight. In this place, under the circumstances it bordered on the ridiculous.

"I am not a child, you know."

"You are a woman . . . an Apache would even brave the dark for a young woman."

"I am not afraid."

"Fear is not a bad thing. It is fear that saves men's lives . . . it prepares a man for trouble."

"How do you come to be here? At this place, I mean? Why did you stop?"

"My horse told me you were there. He also told me you were a woman."

"That's impossible."

"No. My horse does not like the smell of Indians, and he knows that smell, but he likes women because he was raised by a woman who made a pet of him.

"When he stopped I knew it was for a reason, and I had been looking for you. My horse was curious but not afraid, and he looked toward you with his ears up, so I knew you were a white person. Had it been a lion or a wolf he would have indicated it by his fear or by his willingness to fight; and of an Indian he would have been afraid, and pulled away. But he was eager to go toward you, and from that I knew you were a woman."

"You said you had been looking for me?"

"I found your wagon, and figured you would be close by."

"You must be hungry."

"Yes."

"We can offer food, but not much more."

"Wait . . . there will be time enough to eat, but who knows how along it will be again before I talk to a woman in the night?"

Bats swirled in the cool night sky, and a few scattered clouds obscured the stars, and the man on horseback vanished in the greater darkness.

"We saw you earlier today," she said tentatively, as if to test his presence.

"You were on the mountain then," he said.

"Yes . . . we saw Apaches, too."

He offered no explanation, and she valued him the more for this. It was enough that he was here, and must somehow have eluded them. The reason for his presence here at all remained unanswered, and her curiosity prodded her to ask, but she waited, feeling that he would explain in his own time.

"We thought our trail was hidden."

"I have lived among the Shoshones and the Nez Percé." He paused to inhale, then snuffed out his cigarette against a boot and dropped it into the sand. "It is well hidden, but there are trails that do not lie upon the ground."

Beyond the mountains there was a moon, and the sky across the saw-toothed ridges grew pale, long shadows reaching out toward them, darker by reason of the growing paleness from where the moon would be. A faint wind stirred among the mesquite and cedar, a faint testing push of wind that died away almost at once as if it was not worth the effort.

"I may bring trouble," he said then.

"You are followed?"

"Yes."

She accepted that . . . there could be no other reason

for a lone man in this wild land. So he was an outlaw. But who would follow a man into such an area? The Army?

He swung down from his horse and stood still beside the saddle for a moment, feeling a sudden faintness. Then he turned and led the horse toward her. "We had better go in," he said. "I do not trust the night."

He was close to her, and she smelled the staleness of sweat, the smell of horse and old leather, of sage, cedar, and wood smoke. She sensed suddenly that this man was very near to collapse; she could almost feel the tiredness of him.

The thought came to her suddenly as they started to walk inside the canyon. It was a startling, shocking thought but even while she knew it could not be true, she was afraid, and had to ask.

"You aren't . . . you aren't Tom Sanifer?"

"No," he said. "Tom Sanifer is dead. He was killed at Fort Bowie by a man named Adam Stark."

Chapter 5

When he had closed the door behind him he said, "I'm Swante Taggart."

"You'll be wanting to wash," Adam said. "There's water in the bucket, and a basin beside it."

Taggart did not move, but stood, hat in hand, ashamed to invade this quiet place. "No aim to barge in," he said, "only I played out of grub . . . three days back."

Adam noted the size of the man, the faded Army shirt and the worn shotgun chaps. He noted also the hang of the gun and the way the man carried a Winchester as if born with it.

"You've come far."

"I've a man behind me."

"We've asked no questions," Adam said. "You're hungry. You'll eat."

"I can go on . . . I've no right to bring you trouble. That man who's behind me . . . he's the Law."

"You didn't have to tell me that," Adam said quietly. "My sister will get you food."

Taggart dipped up water in the gourd dipper and poured it into the tin basin, liking the sound of it. The bucket was full, the water clear and dark in the shadows at the side of the room, but it was more water than he had seen since he left the Verde.

Miriam put a plate of beef and beans on the table, with a small dish of squaw cabbage, and then brought the blackened pot from the fireplace. As she filled his cup he looked at her hands. They were not dainty, but slender, long-fingered woman's hands, and somehow the seeing of them made him go all quiet inside.

They were gentle hands, strong hands, capable hands; they were the hands of a woman, a mother, a woman to walk beside a man, not behind him.

He looked down at the food before him with sudden helplessness. He bowed his head, not in prayer, but only to prevent their seeing his emotion, and when he picked up his fork he did it almost with reverence. He put a few of the beans into his mouth and began to chew slowly, savoring each taste.

It is only those who have never been hungry who picture a starving man as gorging himself when he first finds food. Taggart was terribly hungry, but he had been so long without food that his stomach had shrunk, and for this first meal he would be able to eat very little. Tomorrow and the next day he would be unable to get enough, but now it was taste he wanted, and flavor. He ate slowly, pausing from time to time to drink great gulps of coffee.

The beans had been baked over a fire of creosote wood and had that extraordinary flavor that only creosote smoke can give. The coffee was strong, hot, and black, and it seemed to bring new strength to him.

After a dozen bites he sat back and rolled a smoke. He felt the eyes of the Mexican girl upon him, dark, magnificent eyes, and she was a woman who made a man conscious of his maleness.

"This is Consuelo," Adam Stark said, "my wife. And,"

he gestured to Miriam, "my sister, Miriam. I am Adam Stark."

Swante Taggart's head came up and Miriam was beside him with the coffee pot and she nudged him slightly. The question half-formed remained unasked.

Adam Stark . . . the man who had killed Tom Sanifer.

Stark had walked into a saloon where Sanifer stood at the bar, and had told him he did not fight before women, but if he wanted to die, to make his fight there. And Tom Sanifer had backed down.

An hour later, when Stark left the saloon, Sanifer had been waiting for him in the dark, but he had missed his first shot. Adam Stark had not.

Taggart put his cigarette on the edge of his coffee saucer and cut off a small bite of the beef. He chewed slowly, taking his time.

"You've had a rough time," Stark said.

"Pete Shoyer is behind me."

"Ah . . . there'll be shooting then."

Taggart emptied his cup. "I've never fired on a badge-wearing man," he said, "but I'll fight if it comes to that."

"Shoyer is a bounty hunter. You'll fight or you'll die."

The candle on the table held a steady light. Miriam filled his cup once more and sat down at the table near him.

He ate a little more, feeling the tenseness leaving his muscles and the quietness come into him, a slow, pleasant, luxurious feeling, dangerous for a man with far to go; but tonight, for this one evening, he would relax.

At the same time his awareness remained with him to the extent that he realized much of what went on here. There were six rifles on the rack in the room, and a shotgun as well; and several boxes covered over in a corner would be ammunition. These people had come to stay, and to defend themselves if attacked. The canyon itself was a little stronghold, and the chances of their being found were slight.

Obviously, from their settled comfort here they had not just come, and they were planning to remain a while longer, and as no cattle were around it had to be mining. Globe was not far south and there was mining there . . . this man had found gold.

He saw no samples in the room, so it must be that Stark was no longer looking for gold; he had found it. And if it was worth staying in this country for, with two women, he had found plenty.

That, then, was why the wagon remained where it had been left, because of the women, and because of the gold he hoped to take out. Gold can be heavy, and he must plan on taking out a lot.

"You can bed down on the floor tonight," Stark suggested. "It is the best we have to offer."

"There are other buildings. It would be best if I slept in one of them . . . in fact, I'd better. I believe Shoyer is far behind, but a man can't know."

"He will not find you," Consuelo said. "Nobody find this place."

"He will find it," Taggart drew in his long legs and got up. "He's a wolf."

"You will be safe here," Consuelo said. "There is danger to go . . . there are Apaches."

He gathered his gear, avoiding the promise in her eyes. "I'm obliged."

Stark rose. "The stable is the place . . . there's hay there. Although you might prefer the chapel."

"A chapel is no place for me," Taggart replied dryly. "I'll take the stable."

Outside, they crossed the narrow space under the stars and went into the darkness of the overhang that shelved above the stable. Taggart spread out a thin bed of hay in the light from the lantern. From where he would lie he could look down the canyon toward the entrance.

"That's scant hay you're using."

Taggart said quietly, "A thin bed makes a light sleeper. I've learned a hard bed sleeps lightly, but safely."

Adam Stark knocked out his pipe on the outside of the door. "If you want to stay on, you're welcome. It's a trying thing to work and worry about this place, although the girls are both handy with guns."

"And Shoyer?"

"Your problem. I'd be offering you nothing but shelter here, and a place to rest up. If you make no tracks, Shoyer can find none."

Taggart stepped outside and went to his horse, who

stood near the pool of water. He had not cared for the horse until he knew he was staying on . . . a man might have to travel fast, and he knew the steeldust would drink. Now he stripped off the saddle and bridle and while the big gelding stood patiently, chewing at a bundle of hay Stark dropped for him, Taggart rubbed the horse down with handfuls of hay.

"You've a neat place here."

"I found it."

"Old Spanish stonework. I've seen it before."

"The Lost Mine of the Padres," Stark said briefly. Only the padres never found it . . . I have."

"I'm not a mining man," Taggart said, "although I've worked mines off and on for others. Started using a single- or double-jack when I was a kid. I'm a cattle-man."

"Own a ranch?"

Swante Taggart stared bleakly into the night, remembering the cabin in New Mexico, the green meadows of hay, the cattle. "I did," he said. "A big outfit moved in and there was trouble."

"Gun trouble?"

"A fair fight, but I beat the wrong man. Now Shoyer is after me."

It happened . . . Adam Stark knew it had happened more than once. It was the day of the cattle baron, not of the small rancher or farmer . . . but he wanted cattle himself.

"I'm no miner, myself," Stark admitted. "Studied geology a little, prospected some. It's cattle I want, and I've a place in mind down Tucson way."

"A man needs water. If he has water he has it all. Longhorns will make a living almost anywhere if they can find water within three days' walk."

"Lots of water on this place I have in mind," Stark said. "Four good water-holes and a small stream. No place on the outfit is more than four miles from water."

"You own it?"

"I can buy it . . . that's why I'm here."

Adam Stark returned to the house, thinking about the ranch. It was a comfort to talk to a man again. Woman-talk was all right, but a man needed men. Suddenly he

45

found himself hoping Taggart would stay on, and if Shoyer came, he could settle that here as well as anywhere. There was no use in a man running.

He went inside . . . Connie was already in bed. Miriam sat by the candle reading.

"What do you think of him?"

Miriam looked up, wondering what to say. "He's a good man, I think."

"I've been trying to remember where I heard that name, and now I know. He rode shotgun on the stage out of Cheyenne to Deadwood."

"Will he stay?"

Adam Stark did not know, and said as much. He pulled off his shirt, thinking about it. If he did stay on he would be a help here, but he must not go up to the mine. If he saw what it was like . . .

He really worried very little about that mine. Anyone might try to go in there, but not one in a million would be foolish enough to swing a pick in there. He just hoped nobody would try it until he was safely out with the hundred thousand he wanted.

Perhaps he had been a fool to tell Taggart so much, but the man was no tenderfoot and he would understand as soon as he looked around in the morning. The old *arrastra* was still there, and no man would be fool enough to remain in such a place unless he had found gold, and lots of it.

Forty miles to the north Pete Shoyer got up from behind a clump of rocks and looked out over the moonlit desert. The horse was still there, standing ground-hitched as he had been for the past hour. By now Shoyer was confident that no one was around.

Behind him in the arroyo where they had taken shelter lay the body of Mark Billings, the last man of the posse he had gathered in Crown King. Until three days ago three men had stayed with him after most of the group had turned back as they started into wilder country.

The four remaining had run into a running fight with Apaches, and of the four only Shoyer remained alive.

One man had been shot from his horse, and the others had holed up in a cave and fought off the Apaches through a day-long battle. At the end of the day one man was dead and Billings wounded.

During the night Shoyer had slipped from under the overhang that formed their cave, and with Billings over his shoulder he had climbed the cliff. Shoyer was a squarely built, powerful man of tremendous strength, and Billings' weight was nothing to him.

When they abandoned their horses for shelter in the cave Shoyer had been afraid they would be found, but they had not. Only one was dead, killed by a stray bullet.

Pete Shoyer knew he was in trouble. In the hard life that lay behind him he had often shaped up with trouble, but this time he knew it would require all his ingenuity to escape from the Apaches, to survive, and carry on to capture Swante Taggart.

He went through the saddlebags and gathered all the food and ammunition on his own horse, as well as the extra canteen. There was a spare pistol now, and he took that and they started off.

Then the Apaches found them again, killed Billings' horse, and shot it out in a bitter fight . . . after which Shoyer got away again, and again took Billings with him. But now Billings, who had done his share in that last fight, had taken two more gunshots. When he died in the arroyo, Shoyer was left alone.

Through that day and part of the night, Pete Shoyer had waited while his water supply ran low, but the Apaches had either given up or drawn off until help was forthcoming. He saw nothing of them, and so, leaving Billings where he had died, but taking his weapons, he mounted up and rode out.

Utilizing all his skill, he attempted to cover his tracks against pursuit, but at the same time he kept pushing ahead. With grudging admiration, he realized at least part of the trouble had been arranged for him by Taggart, who had succeeded in turning attention in the direction from which he had come, and so had left Apaches to watch for his pursuers.

Keeping to lower ground and losing himself in the close-growing ocotillo and mesquite, Pete Shoyer worked his way south, with Rockinstraw Mountain looming against the sky.

On the day Swante Taggart arrived at the canyon of the chapel, Pete Shoyer knew that he himself had evaded pursuit by the Apaches, but had lost the trail of the man he pursued.

He swung back and forth, casting about for the trail, but he found nothing. A mile or two north of the Salt River the trail had just petered out, although for some days past he had been really doubtful if the trail he followed was that of the man he sought. There were differences in the trail and he was hard put to work it out . . . there was an irritating feeling that he had been deceived.

After he crossed the Salt River he rode along the bank for several miles, but found no evidence that anyone had crossed it. He did find the tracks of a party of Apaches, at least a dozen strong, and he felt sure they were the same, now reinforced, who had fought him earlier.

Swante Taggart had disappeared. He had literally dropped off the face of the earth.

But the Apaches had not.

On a rugged shoulder of Squaw Peak, Pete Shoyer studied the terrain and fought his own problem.

He needed supplies. South of him was Globe, and if Taggart had headed south it was to Globe he would go. Meanwhile the Apaches would settle down and forget him. He put his glasses back in the pack and stepped into the saddle. Only a few minutes later Adam Stark emerged from the canyon and started toward Rockinstraw Mountain, the very area Shoyer had been studying a moment before.

For a long time Shoyer stood on his look-out point and surveyed the country around him. It was broken by arroyos, and much of it was covered with desert growth. He realized Taggart could be out there, perhaps only a short distance away, perhaps waiting to kill him.

Pete Shoyer was an officer of the law simply because it could be made to pay well. He did not bother with small fry except for the information they could provide, and his enforcement of the law was devoted to those men for whom large rewards were paid.

He took no joy in killing, nor did he kill unless necessity demanded it, but he thought no more of killing a man than of killing a coyote, a quail, or a pack-rat. As a boy in Texas he had fought Comanches, and had become a skillful sniper, as successful as any Apache at using their tactics.

He cared nothing one way or the other for Taggart. Only Swante Taggart was worth five thousand dollars to him, dead or alive, the reward to be paid by the Bennetts themselves. If he could deliver Taggart alive to the Bennetts they would provide their own hanging, but the problem of taking a prisoner across the country was a tough one.

Some men had to be taken back dead. He preferred it otherwise, because a dead man is mighty hard to load on a saddle each morning, and in hot weather it isn't practical. Moreover, if he took them back alive they might escape and could then be captured again for another reward. Yet to date he had killed nine men, not counting Indians.

Pete Shoyer was a tough man. He had no philosophy of life and had probably never heard the word; certainly he would not have understood it. He had no concealed motivations. He simply hunted men the way he had once hunted buffalo, because it paid well, and for the most part was scarcely more dangerous.

He had grown up hunting. He had hunted rabbits, deer, antelope, lion, bear, and buffalo, and now men. It had begun quite accidentally. A United States Marshal stopping by a cow-camp where he worked had remarked that an outlaw he sought was worth five hundred dollars, dead or alive. Pete Shoyer made a mental calculation as to how many months he must work for five hundred dollars at thirty a month, and decided he was in the wrong business.

He had no desire for a gunman's reputation. He never sought out a dangerous man to challenge to see who was the fastest man; the very idea was ridiculous to him. Who was to gain by such an obviously silly action?

More than once he had gone out of his way to avoid a gun battle. Had he stopped to consider the facts, he would probably have agreed that Swante Taggart was in the right in defending his land, but Pete Shoyer was not interested in who was right. His problem was simplicity itself: a man was wanted, the reward was large, get the man.

His desires were few. He liked women, he liked food, he liked whiskey, although he was never drunk. He liked being Pete Shoyer . . . liked the thought that he never lost a prisoner or a man he once started after. He rarely played cards, because he hated to lose good money . . . it simply made no sense to him. Most of the men who ran the gambling houses were prosperous, and he supposed it was no accident . . . he himself never gave anyone any chances he could avoid giving, and he was sure the gamblers felt the same way.

He had never known what it mean to quit. He trailed men as a beagle trails rabbits, because it was his nature to do so, and he never thought of the right or wrong of it. The men he sought were outlaws; somebody would eventually get them, and it might as well be him.

He was not cruel. He had never needlessly punished anyone. He went about his business as casually as the wind blows. There was no malice toward the men he hunted, unless they had tried to kill him. If they showed signs of fight he usually killed them as the most practical solution.

He had no particular feeling about crime except that most of the criminals he had known were broke. They were always talking about making a big haul, and they lived a poverty-stricken, hunted life while they talked about it.

Their hide-outs were dirty, their blankets filled with bugs, their food cooked in a hurry, their ears sharp for any sound that might mean pursuit. He did much better, and he believed in crime paying, because it paid him.

He understood the minds of the men he trailed, because they were predatory creatures like the wolves, lions, and bears he had hunted earlier. He knew what they wanted and where they had to go to get it. He knew where every sizeable bit of loot was, and kept an eye on these places as a matter of course. He had developed a knowledge of most of the outlaw element, of their friends, relatives, and hide-outs. Most of his jobs were simplicity itself.

The women he liked were the frontier women of the cribs, the ones he could have, pay, and leave behind. He ate, he drank, he had a woman when he felt the need, and from time to time he relaxed and loafed, living a life he could never have afforded by any other means.

He was a dead shot with both rifle and pistol, and when he shot, he shot to kill. He could track as well as any Apache, and it was rarely that he encountered such a problem as Taggart offered.

Not many outlaws would have taken off alone into Apache country. Shoyer felt sure he would find Taggart dead, mutilated, and perhaps beyond identification.

He had lost the trail first when Taggart doubled back through Horsethief Canyon, and he lost it again at the Agua Fria, but he had no idea of giving up: five thousand was the biggest reward he had ever gone after. By the time he discovered that Taggart was heading east into the heart of Apache country, he knew the man he followed was not an ordinary outlaw, nor an ordinary man.

When Pete Shoyer left his lookout near Squaw Peak he rode south for Globe.

But he would be back.

Chapter 6

Swante Taggart awakened suddenly in the dark near the stable door and he lay still, his hand on his gun, listening. Then he heard a door open silghtly. Someone came out and started toward the spring. He listened and heard a faint rustle of skirts.

With sudden embarrassment he realized that in washing the night before, and drinking, he had all but emptied the water bucket and had not refilled it.

He got to his feet and stepped out into the starlit night. For a moment he stood still, testing the night for other sounds, and then after a glance toward the canyon mouth, he started after the girl who had gone for water.

He heard the gulp of the bucket as it took up water, and the falling drops as it was lifted clear, then emptied. Whoever it was, wished to get the bucket thoroughly wet to keep the water cool . . . and then he heard water running into the bucket from the spring itself.

"I'll carry that," he said. "I should have filled it last night."

"You were tired," said Miriam. "Why don't you rest?"

"Not in me, I guess. I'm an early riser."

They stood alone in the darkness, each conscious of the other, each uncertain what to say.

"Does he begin work early?"

"Adam? He tries to get to the mine while it is still dark so he will not be seen moving about. It is something we live with here . . . we try to keep from being seen, or leaving tracks, so we move around as little as possible."

"But you live off the country?"

"Connie knows the plants . . . at least many of them. We use what we can to help with what we brought along. Up the canyon there are some benches that are thickly grown, and on the mountainside above us . . . we're careful."

"She's Indian?"

"Mexican . . . but she grew up with Apaches. She knows them, and she's afraid of them."

He lifted the bucket from the rock and they started back to the cabin. "I'll stay on," he said. "My horse needs a rest."

"And then?"

"Who knows? Maybe I'll ride out of here for Morenci like I planned, but I might turn back to the west. With a man like Pete Shoyer you have to figure mighty careful. He reads a sign like an Apache, and he reads the mind of the man he's chasing. Once you establish a pattern of escape, he'll have it, and he's got you. A man who's running away will nearly always, somewhere along the line, try to double back. He know that. Most times when a man goes into the water to leave no tracks, he'll come out on the same side he goes in."

"I don't see why that should be."

"Neither do I, but it works out that way. So a man on the dodge, he has to out-guess the man on his trail. One time you do it one way, another time another way. Most of all, a man shouldn't try to move fast . . . he should think his way through, do the unexpected several times, then the expected."

"It sounds complicated."

They paused at the door, neither anxious to end this brief exchange, a man and a woman together, standing close in the darkness.

She spoke in a whisper. "What you said about Tom Sanifer . . . was that true?"

"Heard it coming across country. Heard it again in Crown King . . . stories like that get around. I'd say it was true."

"You mustn't say anything about it. . . . We didn't know, Connie and I."

"Story has it a woman was involved."

She looked down at the shine of the dark water in the bucket. "So Adam did it. . . . I'm not surprised."

He opened the door and they stepped into the room. There was a rustle of movement from the further room, and he put the bucket up on the table against the wall where the gourd hung. Only a candle glowed in the silent room.

He knelt at the fireplace and stirred the few coals, banked with ashes against the night just passed. And then he added a few twigs, a piece of bark, some mesquite wood. A flame curled around the mesquite, shooting out a red tongue toward the willingness of the bark. Swante Taggart looked up at the girl standing near him. Their eyes met, and he looked quickly back at the fire, then got up and turned toward the door.

"I'll have coffee in a few minutes."

"All right."

He closed the door softly behind him and crossed to the stable. Habitually, when unable to undress because of the circumstances, he wore moccasins instead of boots. They were comfortable, didn't make his feet swell as the boots were apt to do, and were better for moving quietly if he had to get up in the night.

Now he went to the horse and put more feed before him, talked to him a few minutes, and led him to water. When he returned him to his feed he checked the position of his saddle and left his rifle by the door jamb where he could put a hand on it instantly.

The canyon was gray now . . . everything was visible, although there was no sun yet in the sky, and a few stars still hung like late lanterns in the early light.

He stood for a time listening, and then he walked down to the mouth of the canyon. There, keeping under cover, he took a long time studying the country, not only with an eye to seeing any sign of Shoyer or Apaches, but to know every draw, every bluff, every obstacle he might have to evade or use. Two-thirds of any fight was a knowledge of terrain, and he intended to be ready when and if the time came.

At breakfast they ate in silence. When they had finished, Stark looked over the coffee cup at him. "You're staying on?"

"A while."

"Good."

Stark pushed back from the table. "Miriam will show you the way up Rockinstraw when there's time . . . we try to keep out of sight and make as little noise as possible. When there's Indians about, we make no sound at all, and have no fires. Otherwise, we try to keep a fair watch from the top of Rockinstraw."

When Stark had gone Taggart went outside. Consuelo glanced after him, and then looked at Miriam. "I think you like him."

"I don't know him," Miriam protested.

Consuelo was right . . . and how long had it been since she was excited about a man?

"He is a fighter," Consuelo said. "He is not like Adam."

"What do you know of Adam?" Miriam was suddenly angry. "You know nothing of him at all. What makes a man is inside him."

"What Adam has inside I don't know," Consuelo replied. "He let Tom Sanifer tell him. Right in front of me, Tom Sanifer told him what he would do, and Adam sat there, just sat there! What would Adam do if Tom Sanifer came here after me?"

"He'd run him off or kill him," Miriam replied, "and if he didn't, I would." She paused, considering it. "And anybody like him," she added. "You're a fool, Connie, not to realize that you've married a good man, a fine man, but you're like a child grasping at a lot of tinsel and glitter because you've never had it. Believe me, it will

54

crumble away in your hands and you'll have nothing left . . . nothing."

"I think of this," Consuelo replied soberly, "but I am empty inside for things I want to know. What does a woman have? Much trouble always, a little laughter, a little dancing, a little crying, and a little time in bed with a man, and then she die. I have never play. I want to laugh, I want to hear music, I want to be gay." Consuelo paused. "I want something before I die."

"There's children."

"Yes. I think of that. But I think I am bad girl. I want a strong man to take me. I don't care if he hurt me if he is strong. Adam, he is good man, but he was afraid of Tom Sanifer.

"Adam talks of tomorrow, but how do I know if to-morrow comes? How do I know what happen? I want to wear pretty dresses I do not make. I want to eat meals I do not cook. I want to get out of bed and not have to think of making the bed. I do not want to think about tomorrow."

"Tomorrow comes whether you think about it or not."

"I am fool. I know tomorrow comes, but if today I have what I want . . . I do not care."

"Do you think Tom Sanifer could have given you any-thing? Or would even have tried?"

"Tom Sanifer told Adam he will come for me, and Adam does nothing. What kind of a husband is *that?*"

Should she tell her? Miriam hesitated, wanting nothing so much as to tell her, but more important, she realized suddenly, was for Consuelo to discover for herself what kind of man she had married. Yet Miriam could not leave the subject entirely.

"Why did Adam go to Fort Bowie, that time?"

Consuelo turned, her dark eyes flashing. "Because he was afraid! He was afraid Tom Sanifer come back!"

"Maybe not," Miriam replied.

"I do not care," Consuelo replied, "I want to go. I am 'fraid. Every day I am afraid, and every night. If Adam will not take me, I will go alone. Or," her eyes flashed, "I get Señor Taggart to take me!"

Miriam felt her spine stiffen with a sharp anger, but

she did not turn around. Her back was to Consuelo and she kept it that way, but deep inside her there was a terrible sinking feeling. She knew what effect Consuelo had on men, for she had seen it, and none of them were indifferent to her, or could be indifferent. She had a fine body, and those magnificent eyes, and she knew how to appeal to men.

"Why do you think he stayed?" Consuelo said. "You think it was because of *you?*"

Miriam remembered the quiet talk in the darkness and suddenly she knew she loved Swante Taggart. It was nonsense . . . how could she love a man she scarcely knew? But out there in the night there had been something, some meeting between them. Yet how could that be, when he had not even seen her then?

"I think he stayed because he wanted to stay," Miriam replied evenly. "I think he will go when he wishes to go, but I do not believe he will take another man's wife."

"Hah!" Consuelo snorted. "You think so? You fool, you."

Swante Taggart walked away from the house. He carried a rifle, field glasses, and canteen and he went up the canyon back of the chapel where the canyon walls seemed to shoot straight up toward the sky. Then he began to climb over boulders, and twice had to pull himself up sheer faces eight or ten feet high. Presently he left the canyon and climbed out on the side.

He was well up, southeast of Rockinstraw, and with a good view of the country except where it was cut off by the bulk of Rockinstraw itself. Seating himself in the shade of a thick cedar, he put his rifle across his lap and got out the glasses. For an hour he studied the terrain.

It was a good place to hide.

Swante pushed his hat back on his head and rolled a smoke, his eyes squinting as he looked around. North of him lay the country he had crossed to get here, and south of him he believed he could almost detect a thin trail of smoke that might be Globe . . . in this clear air a man could see a long way.

Nowhere was there any sign of Adam Stark or his

workings. Probably he was deep in a canyon some place, and well out of sight.

His thoughts returned to the two girls. That Mexican girl now . . . that was a lot of woman. There was something going on he did not understand, and apparently Stark had told neither of them that he had killed this Sanifer. Could be why he had rushed them away into the desert, so they would not hear.

Miriam had not seemed upset over it . . . she had even seemed pleased, so she couldn't have been the woman.

But she wouldn't have been. Miriam was the kind of girl who would go with a man if she wanted to, and not be ashamed of it, but he'd have to be quite a man. She was a proud one . . . but all woman, too.

A chaparral cock ran across the slope before him, stopping to flip a tail at him and eye him inquisitively. Overhead a buzzard soared against the sky, and in the distance, over the mountains, billowing black clouds were piling up. The drouth had been long . . . it was one of the driest years in some time, and a good rain would put water along the trails. And it would erase, once and for all, any tracks he might have left.

Even here, only a few yards from the rim of the canyon of the chapel, he could scarcely see it. The padres had chosen their hiding place very well indeed.

But Swante Taggart was not safe, and he was not free. He knew better than to relax and forget his situation. Pete Shoyer was not likely to give up a chase that would prove so profitable. Even if for a time he took on something else, it would only be to return to the pursuit of Taggart when time allowed.

Taggart got up and moved across the slope, ignoring the sharp warning of a rattler a dozen feet off the trail. The snake was coiled in the shade where he had better be . . . a few minutes of direct sunlight in such heat as this would kill any rattlesnake.

Twice rabbits started up . . . he would set some snares away from the canyon. Once he saw deer tracks.

He caught a slight movement on the hill below him and stood still until he identified it as Consuelo. She had a hand-woven basket and was collecting seeds or something from desert plants. She moved with easy grace, like an Indian girl, but he could see she was wary. Suddenly, he was sure she was aware of his presence. Had she seen him first?

The thought was not a comfortable one to a man who must survive by never being seen first if he could avoid it, and he settled down to watch her.

There was an animal grace about her, and when he had looked into her eyes the night before there had been a challenge there. This was quite a woman . . . but she was also a danger.

He lifted his eye to the far slope of the mountains but saw nothing. Slowly his eyes moved around the hills, seeking out every possible way of travel, searching for any indication of movement. The clouds were building higher . . . it might actually rain.

He got up in one swift, lithe movement and went down the hill toward Consuelo.

She had turned her back on him but he knew she was aware of his coming. No stones rattled under his feet. He stepped lightly and easily. Even the Apache moccasins, which were harder of sole than the moccasin of the Plains Indians, allowed a chance to feel what was beneath the feet. An Indian never allowed his weight to come down on a branch or twig.

Once, Swante Taggart paused to look around the country again. The buzzard still circled. There was a touch of wind in the air, a breath of cooling wind that smelled of rain. In the distance lightning flashed, and thunder rumbled in the far-off canyons and tossed great balls of sound back and forth among the peaks.

He walked on down the slope of the mountain and paused near Consuelo. "You'd better get back," he said. "There's a storm coming."

"I like it."

The wind blew her skirt around her ankles and she lifted her head to the oncoming storm, letting it blow her black hair back from her neck and face. She wore a loose blouse that left her neck and smooth brown shoulders bare.

Lightning flashed in the dark clouds in the west, and

the wind touched the violin of the cedars and hummed softly among the spines of the *cholla*. Far away on the mountainside a gray veil of rain appeared briefly, then vanished as the brief shower died . . . a warning of what was to come.

Taggart scanned the middle distance, searching for movement. The air was startling in its clarity, and the weirdly lit sky made the desert and the mountains seem strangely unreal, like some enchanted moonscape of crater and serrated ridge.

They stood together in silence, drawn closer by the coming storm, rapt in their attention to the strangeness of the mountains. It would wipe out tracks . . . this he remembered, and praised the storm even when he was not sure what else might come of it.

If Pete Shoyer was out there now he must be hunting shelter, but Taggart saw nothing, heard nothing.

"It comes fast, I think," Consuelo said, but she made no move to go. He stood quietly beside her.

"You go soon?" she asked suddenly.

"A few days, a week . . . maybe more. I do not know yet."

"You are lucky. I hate it here . . . *I hate it!*"

Taggart made no reply, watching the black thunderheads billowing up in vast cloudy castles, ominous and threatening, and beneath them the advancing legions of the rain. "It is time to go," he said, and taking her elbow started down the mountain.

After a few steps the demands of the trail drew them apart, and he was careful not to come close to her again. They went down the slope, half-walking, half-running, excited by the oncoming storm and the hurry for shelter.

Once, pausing for breath on a narrow ledge before starting down an edge of trail into the canyon itself, Consuelo turned her dark eyes on him. "I think I go soon. I have feeling . . . if I stay here, I die here. I am 'fraid."

She went down the trail ahead of him, and with a last look around he hurried down into the canyon. When they reached the door of the stone house a few scattered drops were already falling, and as they ducked inside the rain swept down with a roar.

These mountain rains, he knew, were usually swift and short, but sometimes they lasted longer. And where was Adam in all this fierce downpour?

He had noted Miriam's quick glance from one to the other as they rushed in the door. "What about Stark?" he asked. "Is there shelter out there?"

"There's a cliff dwelling not far off . . . just an overhang faced with rock, but it's dry." Miriam was busy at the fire. "He will be all right. Adam probably saw the storm coming before any of us."

"We were high up," Swante Taggart said. "We saw nobody riding . . . not anywhere around."

He thought of the trail over which he had come. Whatever else happened, there'd be no tracks now for Shoyer, but how close was he? Had he trailed him as far as the Salt River? If he had, he would be close enough to observe movement in the country around, and he was a man with the patience of an Indian.

Taggart sat down and Miriam placed a cup of coffee before him. He stared at it, thinking of Consuelo. There was no telling what she had in mind, but everything about her was a challenge to his maleness. Every move was provocative, every glance a testing of him. It excited him, but it worried him too, for his good sense told him how explosive the situation was. There was something between the two women that set a man's teeth on edge . . . no declared war, but a guarded antagonism that he sensed with every instinct he had. As for Adam Stark, he knew those slow-smiling, quiet men. And he was in no position to invite trouble. The best he could get would be the worst of it.

He had been a fool to stay, yet there was no way he could have gone on. The solution now was to get out, and fast. He made up his mind suddenly. When the storm was over, he was going to go.

The roar of rain on the roof drowned the opening of the door, but the sudden brush of damp air turned Taggart sharply around.

Pete Shoyer stood in the doorway and he had a hand on his gun.

"Hello, Taggart," he said.

Chapter 7

For an instant the tableau was frozen in silence. Pete Shoyer loomed square and black in the gray light of the doorway, his features indistinguishable. He seemed in that moment as solid and indestructible as a mountain boulder, as ominous as destiny itself. His sudden appearance from out of the storm, his featureless presence, the square blackness of his outline in the storm-darkened room was somehow shocking and terrible.

Yet in that moment it was to Taggart that Miriam's eyes went, and he stood very tall and still in the half-light of the room, at once ready and at ease.

One wrong move could shatter the darkness of the room with the lightning flash of a gun battle, and Miriam heard herself speaking quietly. "Come in. We've coffee on."

"I don't mind if I do." Shoyer stepped into the room and his face showed clearly then, wide, dark, somber. He had large eyes that seemed to see everything at once. He was worn and stained, and on his shirt there was a stain of old blood. His slicker was open and the firelight caught the reflection of the brass cartridges in his belt, which glowed like golden teeth.

Pete Shoyer moved into the room and coolly removed his slicker and hung it on a peg, his hat over it. Swante Taggart had moved slightly to face him as he changed position, but had said nothing.

When he turned from the coat peg Shoyer looked at Taggart. "I've come to take you in, Taggart," he said.

"When you try," Taggart's voice was dispassionate, "I'll kill you."

Shoyer showed his teeth in a wide smile. "Nobody has," he replied, and then he said to Miriam. "You spoke of coffee, ma'am. I can use it."

Miriam, caught by the moment, the meeting of hunter

and hunted, had forgotten the coffee. "Oh . . . yes." She brought the pot to the table, and a cup.

Shoyer drew back a chair and seated himself. "You've led me a chase."

"I don't like to kill a man wearing a badge. I've worn one myself."

"So I've heard." Shoyer gulped coffee noisily, then poured the hot coffee into his saucer and blew on it. "Need be no killing. You just come along quiet."

"We'll decide that when the time comes."

Both turned their heads as the door opened and Stark came in. His smile was friendly, with a hint of irony. "I see you've met," he said.

He hung up his slicker and dried off his rifle barrel before racking it. "Had my rifle on you coming up the draw," he told Shoyer. "I thought you were an Apache."

"You were behind me?" Shoyer did not like the idea.

"All the way from the river."

Shoyer's eyes swept the room, assaying the situation carefully, not sure what he had stepped into here. Suspicion was hot in his dark, slow eyes.

Taggart made matters clear. "These people took me in, as they have you. What happens here concerns only you and me. I would not want you to make a mistake."

"We'll see."

Taggart spooned honey into his coffee. "When this storm is over, why don't you just ride out of here?"

"You're worth too much money to me, Taggart. Alive or dead." He sipped coffee from the saucer and wiped the back of his hand across his mouth. "Anyway, I can't ride out. My horse broke a leg last night or I'd be in Globe by now."

"How did you find this place?" Stark asked.

"Now that's a coincidence," Shoyer explained agreeably. "A man in my business makes a point of marking down in his memory such places where a man might hide. One time when I was scouting for the Army I almost fell into this canyon, but until I needed a place I had clean forgotten it."

"You stirred something up," Stark said. "You've got the Apaches out and hunting. My advice is that nobody try to leave here until things simmer down. When they get out like this they prowl like hungry wolves, and I've the women to think of."

Shoyer tipped back in his chair. "Suits me." He put a toothpick between his teeth. "Dry place to sleep, women folks to do for a man . . . can't say I'd mind a rest."

Outside the rain pounded on the roof, and Consuelo had put a pot under a leak in the roof. Occasionally a huge drop fell into the water already gathered there, the sound loud in the silent room.

Only a trickle of water ran down the floor of the canyon, and the presence of the buildings there after all these centuries indicated that there was rarely more at any time. A flash flood would have torn out the stable and damaged the other buildings. The deep canyons and washes that scarred the desert were carved out by just such flash floods that would run bank full for a few hours and then vanish. But in those few hours, or even in minutes, dams could be ripped out and homes destroyed.

Swante Taggart watched the rain flooding past the window and rolled a smoke. From this moment he would have no rest, knowing Pete Shoyer's reputation for bringing in his man, yet he was not excited or even worried. His years had taught him that each problem was to be met when it approached, and nothing was to be done about such situations until the moment for action. His problem now was simply to wait . . . and to be on guard for any sudden move that Shoyer might make.

He had no fear of Shoyer. He had been shot at before this, and with luck he would come out of this to be shot at again. If not, he would be dead and it would not matter anyway. He was neither a fool nor an egotist, but he knew what he could do with a gun, and the years had keyed his muscles and mind for emergencies. He lived on a plane of readiness and awareness.

He had never considered himself a gunfighter, and had never drawn a gun unless necessity demanded. He had tried to avoid gun trouble as a man avoids grass fires, stampedes, or flash floods, simply because it was the intelligent thing to do. At the same time, when such troubles did come he believed they should be met head-on and moving in.

Swante Taggart had never thought of himself as a

brave man. The very word made him restless and irritable when it came into a conversation, as if men could be divided into the brave and the cowardly, as if brave men were always brave and the cowards always cowardly. It simply wasn't that way. A man did what he had to do.

Considering Shoyer, Taggart did not think of the man as either a good or bad character. The man hunted men. So he hunted men? If Pete Shoyer wanted to make a business out of hunting men, it was alright with Taggart. Some men hunted buffalo, some hunted wolves . . . hunting men was infinitely more dangerous. There were some who thought such conduct evil . . . Taggart himself did not.

Perhaps there was something in Pete Shoyer that carried the hunting somewhat further than a man should go. Possibly he was too intent . . . Taggart was unconcerned about that. Whatever else he was, Pete Shoyer was a tough man who knew his business, and he would neither be trapped, tripped up, or tricked out of his prisoner by an ordinary ruse. If it came to shooting, Pete Shoyer would want the edge. But Taggart was pretty sure Shoyer would avoid a shoot-out.

Not that Shoyer was afraid. It simply was not good business, for Shoyer might be wounded himself and unable to take his prisoner or pursue him. Shoyer was no reputation-proud kid, nor was he a tenderfoot. He was simply a man-hunter who was good at his job.

Stark turned from the window and for an instant Taggart caught his face in the light and was struck by its tautness, something he had not observed before. As he watched Stark he realized the man had lost weight, his eyes seemed hollow. It was odd, for Stark seemed to be a bear for strength, one of those resilient men, hard and tough, who seem capable of enduring anything.

Something was wrong, but it was not his domestic troubles. Studying the man, Taggart became thoroughly engrossed. During the brief period since his arrival in the canyon of the chapel there had been barely time to become acquainted, but Taggart was a sensitive man, aware as an animal of the subtle antagonisms of those around him. But this was something more, and it worried him because he sensed that Stark himself was worried.

Miriam gathered up the dishes, busy with her own thoughts. Consuelo sat quietly sewing, working over a shirt of Adam's. Only once in a while her black eyes flashed at Taggart. Shoyer was aware of it, and a gleam of amusement tinged with jealousy showed in his dark eyes.

Stark got out a deck of cards and dealt solitaire. Taggart stood up and shrugged into his slicker. Shoyer watched him.

"You goin' some place?"

"So?"

"I'll go along." Shoyer got up. "You and me, we're goin' to be mighty close."

He glanced around at Stark. "How about sellin' me a horse? Then I can take this gent out of here and be off your hands."

Adam Stark puffed on his pipe and studied the cards thoughtfully before he replied.

"No," he said, "I'll not sell you a horse. I'll lend you one when the time is right for you to move, but until then you get nothing, and if you take a horse without my permission I'll have the law on you."

"I am the law."

Stark glanced up and puffed on his pipe, then took it from his teeth. "Not to me, you aren't. You're a man who makes his living hunting men. Furthermore," he glanced at the cards, "I am not sure you have any authority in this Territory."

Pete Shoyer sat up abruptly. "I'll have you know—"

Stark lifted a hand. "Understand me. I'm not denying your right to make arrests, but I am not sure you have that right here. If I were you I'd go very slow. I'd want to be sure what the governor of the Territory has to say about such action. As I understand it, the shooting you want this man for took place in New Mexico?"

"It did."

"Been my experience," Stark said calmly, "that the Arizona folks look with some understanding upon a shooting where one man is attacked by several and comes out ahead. I think you'd have a time getting this man out of Arizona."

Shoyer chuckled. "You let me worry about that. This

man is wanted. I don't care what he's wanted for, or what the facts were. That's up to the judge and jury."

Swante Taggart ignored the discussion. He opened the door, and stepped out into the rain. The trickle of water down the canyon floor had swelled to a fair-sized stream, but he sprang over it and crossed to the barn. Leading his horse to water, he saw Pete Shoyer come to the door wearing a slicker. The man-hunter stood there within the shelter of the rain, watching as Taggart watered the horse and then returned it to the barn, where he filled the manger with hay.

There was only a little fodder such as they would have been able to gather on the hills and in the few meadows around. Only enough for a day or two. Taggart went to the door of the barn and looked at the rain. The door of the house opened and Miriam came out and crossed to him.

They stood together watching the rain. "What are you going to do?" she asked at last.

"Stay on. I said I would, and I'm through running."

"And if he tries to take you?"

"I hope he doesn't."

"He frightens me. There's something about him . . . I mean, he seems indomitable, somehow. You look at him and you can't imagine anyone or anything standing against him."

"He's done pretty well."

"If I can help, I will." She hesitated. "There's a way out of the canyon when you get back up against the mountain. A man on foot could get out of there, and if he could get over behind that pointed peak southeast of here . . . well, I could bring a horse over there."

"Stay out of it."

"But what are you going to do?"

"Wait." The house door stood slightly open and he knew Shoyer was within, watching them. "No use hunting trouble. I'm going to sit tight and let him make his move . . . and then I'll do what needs to be done."

"I think he'll try to kill you."

"His way." He leaned out to study the sky. The clouds overhead were low, heavy, bulging with rain. "What

about you? What are you going to do? With your life,
I mean."

She looked around at him. "What does anyone do?
I'll live it as it comes."

"And when you get out of here?"

She countered with her own question. "What will *you*
do? You've said something about a ranch . . . is that
just talk, or do you have plans?"

He stared gloomily into the afternoon. "I had plans. I
even had a ranch, and then a hard-nosed bunch came
riding in from Texas and I shot myself out of it. Out of
my ranch and into trouble."

He built a smoke, taking his time. "To tell you the
truth, I don't know. Maybe I'll stop here in Arizona, or
I might go west to California. And that's as much as I
know."

"Why don't you talk to Adam? He doesn't know as
much about cattle as he'd like. You two might make a
team."

"Has Stark got a horse to spare? I mean to loan him?"

"There's one. Not a very good horse."

"The two of us could ride out of here together. Shoyer
and me . . . and we could settle it out there, somewhere.
Get out of your hair."

"Don't do it."

The rain was letting up, although the clouds were
still heavy and the water in the bottom of the canyon
held to a steady flow. There was a dam upstream where
some of it could be held against dry weeks to furnish
water for the horses and to bring the grass in the hollow
into better condition.

"I never wanted trouble with any man," Taggart said
suddenly. "But if a fellow comes at you, what can you
do?"

"I know."

"They judge a man out here by his honesty and his
courage, and it's right they should. Most ways a man
can go in this country he goes into danger, so you want
a man alongside you who has guts. You don't want to
start a wagon across the trails with a coward who'll quit
the first time you run into trouble . . . he'll get you
killed.

"And if you're doing business out here, a man's word has to be good. We don't have lawyers and courts to decide, and we don't have a lot of legal nonsense to go through. If I buy cattle from a man and he tells me he's got ten thousand head, there'd better be ten thousand head . . . but there will be. No need to count 'em.

"That's why if a man is called a coward or a liar it's a shooting matter. Nobody wants to associate or do business with either. Man can't afford to let folks call him either one."

Swante Taggart stepped out of the doorway and looked around at the sky. In the west the clouds were piled up against the mountains, but the wind had changed and the clouds overhead were breaking up.

"There's pushy folks around this country, and if they start pushing you, you have to push back. If you don't, they'll soon push you out of the country."

They stood silent for a few minutes and then Swante Taggart said quietly, "You'd better say something to your brother. A man who'll hunt down and kill a man for a couple of hundred dollars might decide it was worth while to kill one for a gold mine."

"You think he knows?"

"He knows. He may even know where the mine is. Pete Shoyer may be a killing man but he's no fool."

Chapter 8

At daybreak Swante Taggart, wearing moccasins, slipped out of the barn where he had slept and went up the canyon, easily finding the place of which Miriam had told him. He climbed out and from a vantage point behind a clump of cedar he studied the country with infinite care.

Shoyer had seen him go, but knew he was helping with the grub problem and he had seen that Taggart took no horse. And without a horse in this country a man just was not going anywhere at all. Had Shoyer known

Taggart better he would not have felt so sure, for the rancher was a man who had grown up hunting on foot and, like an Apache, he could travel farther in a day on his feet than on a horse.

Stark believed the Apaches were still around, and Taggart was prepared to go along with Stark. Although not long in the west, Stark was an observant man, with an uncanny grasp and a feeling for the West and for Indians. Such a man was worth a dozen more experienced but less observing men.

Yet Stark had gone out that morning after originally planning to do nothing of the kind, and Taggart was both curious and worried about the older man.

Not even the girls knew the exact location of the mine, Taggart believed, or if they did they were saying nothing, but their very lack of knowledge had aroused Taggart's curiosity, for Stark was a man who trusted his women folks, and if he had kept the site secret from them he did so for a reason.

Swante Taggart had been doing some thinking on his own, and from his conclusions it seemed likely that the mine was at least three miles and perhaps a little more from the canyon of the chapel . . . somewhere in the rugged country east of the Horseshoe Bend of the Salt.

For half an hour he studied the terrain, but he saw no movement or evidence of life. Then keeping to rock ledges, or stepping from stone to stone where possible, Taggart worked his way across country. That several canyons emptied into the Salt from the east and southeast he already knew from his observations north of the river before coming to the canyon.

He was more than two hours traveling less than four miles, for he had taken cover from time to time to check both his back trail and the country around.

Everywhere the rain had washed out tracks, washed the air clean, and left the country looking fresh and new. A snake had crossed a small sand bed . . . there were the tracks of a lizard, and a place where a covey of quail had raced along the ground in a wide group. Otherwise, he saw no tracks of any kind.

He heard the sound of a pick before he located Stark. When he heard the sound he took cover and looked about for the mine, but he saw nothing that even faintly resembled a working of any kind. The sound had momentarily stopped, and he lay still.

To the south of him and a little west was a pinnacle of rock that loomed up like a beckoning finger, and the mountainside sloped steeply away below it. Taking his Winchester in hand, Taggart started down the slope, and then he heard the sound of the pick again. A blow . . . another blow.

Swante Taggart paused and felt a sudden prickling along his scalp. He had heard a faint stirring in the rock such as one heard sometimes in the stope of a mine. The sound was similar to that of timbers taking weight deep underground, and it was a sound he had never liked.

He went on down the slope and paused again. Before him the pinnacle of rock leaned ever so slightly down slope. At the very base of it a deep notch had been cut into the underpinning of the pinnacle.

He looked at the rock tower and saw that it was seamed with ancient cracks and cleavages. The rock had no coherence; it looked shattered and broken. As he watched, Adam Stark crawled from the notch dragging a sack. When he straightened up he saw Taggart.

For an instant the two men stared at each other, and then Stark relaxed slowly. "Found me," he said. "Well, you've done some mining."

Taggart walked past him, looking up at the tower. His mouth felt dry and he was breaking out in a cold sweat. The very idea of going into that notch under the tower sent a chill through every fiber of his body.

"You're crazy," he said flatly. "Stark, any man who would work in a place like that has got to be crazy."

"The gold is there."

Taggart turned and looked at him. "You don't want gold that bad. Nobody does, nobody in his right mind."

Adam took out his pipe and began to fill it. "A matter of viewpoint, Taggart. How bad does a man want anything? I guess it all depends on the man, and what he wants and why. I know what I'm doing. I know what my chances are. I know that in that gold there's a ranch, there's cattle, there's comfort for my wife. There's a trip for her . . . to San Francisco. Maybe even to Europe."

"And you can die in there."

"That's right."

They were silent. Adam Stark lighted his pipe. In the morning light his face looked drawn and gray, and Taggart could appreciate the strain he must be under, working in such a place.

"That's why you've kept the girls away."

"That's why." Stark squatted on his heels, his eyes searching the country around, from old habit. "Look, Taggart, two weeks more in there, and I'll have it made."

"Two *weeks?*"

"The stuff is richer now than it ever was. Look." Stark took a chunk of ore from the sack. "Just look at that."

"I—" Swante Taggart swallowed his words. The ore was jewelry story rock, the kind a man hears about all his life and rarely, if ever, sees. It was heavy, so heavy that the weight of it startled him, and he was used to gold. The rock was seamed with streaks of gold, not the hairlike threads in some ore, but bands of it. And the quartz was rotten. His fingers broke off chunks of it and there was crumbling from the pressure of his fingers.

Swante Taggart was not a man who loved gold, but he knew the feeling. It could get into the blood, and once it did a man was lost. He had known men who devoted their entire lives to following the ghost of gold through desert and mountain, into all the lost and remote places. He could appreciate the feeling, although he had long since come to realize there were some things not worth the cost. For him the yearning was for land, cattle, a place with water, trees, and grass.

But for gold like this there was little a man wouldn't do. Yet Adam Stark was not really filled with gold lust, either, and was as well-balanced a man as Taggart had ever seen.

"Sure," Taggart said, "it's rich. I've never seen the like. But why, when the risk is so great? All of that gold won't buy you six months of life, or even a day of it."

"No."

"Then it's the women?"

Adam nodded. "It's Connie. Not Miriam . . . she's like I am or you are. She's a girl who can make out, and

71

she asks nothing of life she can't get. But Miriam's had a nice time behind her, something Connie's never had, and Connie has a restlessness in her. I think a spell of real living would cure her."

"You're wrong."

Stark looked at him.

"She says that's what she wants," Taggart went on, "and she believes it. After a fashion I suppose she does, but what she really wants is to believe in you."

"That's up to her."

Swante Taggart indicated the rock by a jerk of his head. "You should let her see that."

"No."

"And you shouldn't let Shoyer see it."

"How about you?" Stark looked at him with a faint smile. "You've seen it."

"It's your gold, and anybody who would dig it out of there is entitled to it. But if I were you," Taggart grinned, "I'd even watch me. A man with that kind of gold can't afford to trust anyone."

The morning sun warmed the mountainside. In the far distance the Four Peaks lost themselves against the sky. Below, the mountain fell away toward the Salt River, scarcely a mile away.

"Why don't you tell her that you killed Sanifer?"

Stark stared at him. "You heard of that?"

"She'd like you for it."

"Maybe . . . and she might hate me. She's made a big thing of him in her mind." Stark lit his pipe again. "Nothing much to him, really. A flashy big man with an easy way of talking, but no sand . . . no bottom to the man, not when the showdown came."

He paused and a slow minute passed. "He wouldn't fight me. He backed down cold when I braced him in the saloon, and then when I started to leave, he tried to dry-gulch me."

"She'll hear of it."

"I'd rather not." Stark got up and knocked out his pipe. Suddenly he no longer felt like smoking. "There's things she has to learn for herself. If she doesn't learn them, there's nothing more to be said."

The air was clear following the storm. Silence lay like

72

a blessing upon the land and the warm sun burned off the last of the night's chill. High overhead an eagle cried and sunlight sparkled on the waters of the Salt. The Apaches came out of a draw on the north side of the river and walked their horses through the sparse growth toward the river bank. There were at least thirty of them and they had several extra horses. They drew up at the river bank and looked the country over. Taggart sat very still, hearing his heart pound. He knew that Stark saw them, too.

If they rode into the water and along the westernmost arm of Horseshoe Bend they would emerge from the river where the dim trail led up Mud Springs Wash between Rockinstraw Mountain and the canyon of the chapel. If Miriam had gone from the canyon to the top of Rockinstraw this morning, they would find her tracks.

"It's a one-man job," Taggart said. "I'll circle around and get on the mountain near the canyon. I can see them, and I'll know it if they find her tracks."

"One against thirty?"

"One man can do as much as two in this case. If both of us got it, that would leave the girls with Shoyer . . . or the Apaches."

Taggart went over back of the slope and as soon as he was below the crest, he started to run. He ran lightly and easily. If the Apaches followed the route, he thought they would have a little less distance to go than he himself.

He ran easily, with long, steady strides. The slope was steep and rocky, but a barely discernible game trail skirted the hill well below the crest. Slowing down to cross a wash, he got a glimpse of the Apaches as they rode down the river, keeping to the edge of the water. He turned up a canyon that led south and came out of it to climb the mountain near the canyon.

From the mountainside above the canyon, overlooking the trail up Mud Springs Wash, Swante Taggart had a good field of fire. Squatting on his heels behind a juniper, he watched the Indians, still some distance off.

They were moving slowly and studying the bank, obviously searching for indications of a crossing. Taggart had deduced from the dried blood on Shoyer's shirt that there had been a battle . . . and now the Indians were out in force to hunt the hunter.

From where he crouched he could see into the canyon; the spring and its pool were visible, and one shoulder of the old chapel. As he watched, Miriam came into sight, and picking up a rock, he tossed it into the pool. She turned quickly and looked up.

He indicated the canyon mouth and flashed his ten fingers at her three times. Instantly, Miriam turned and ran for the house.

Whatever else he might be, Shoyer was a fighting man and good to have along at this time, for Taggart had a hunch the Indians were not going to pass on.

When the Apaches rode up to Mud Springs they were stretched out for a hundred yards or more, but at the springs they dismounted and scattered out, searching for indications that the spring had lately been used.

It was one place that was carefully avoided by all at the canyon of the chapel . . . but what about Shoyer? Had he stopped there? And if he had, had the rain washed out all traces?

From his position on the slope of the hill, Taggart could cover the approach to the mouth of the canyon, but he could not see what was happening inside the mouth where Shoyer or one of the girls was sure to be waiting.

The edge of the canyon at this point was broken by several deep cracks, and slabs of rock lay scattered in profusion. Mingled among them were juniper and prickly pear, and the position allowed some movement under concealment.

One by one the Apaches drifted back to Mud Springs, evidence enough that they had found no tracks. If one of the girls had gone to the mountain this morning they must certainly have left some indication, so evidently Consuelo as well as Miriam was in the canyon.

The Apaches were making camp now, but several of them mounted and rode off, obviously scouting for Shoyer. It was very early, far too early for an Apache to camp unless there was reason for remaining in the vicinity . . . and this was a war party. Without doubt they had reason to believe him in the vicinity, and remember-

ing how many tracks there must be on top of Rockinstraw, Taggart prayed they would not climb the lookout
mountain.

He built a cigarette, continuing to watch the Indians.
There would be a fight, he was sure of that. Somehow
they would find the canyon, or signs of the presence of
some of the party, and then there would be some shooting. He had seen Apaches fight before, and he had
fought them, just as he had fought Kiowas, Comanches,
Sioux, and Modocs. He remembered the smoky smell of
their bodies, the swiftness with which they could run,
the suddenness with which they could disappear. With
Apaches a man had to shoot first and think later.

With a kind of sour respect, he watched them make
their search. There seemed nothing methodical about it,
and yet he knew nothing could have been more thor-
ough. Only the rain had saved them thus far.

By now Adam Stark would probably have returned to
the canyon and would be ready for trouble. And Shoyer
was there. Three men and two women, and their position
was good, but he knew that he would not give much for
their chances at this moment. If he had been elsewhere
and had been asked how long three men and two women
could survive against thirty Apaches, he would have
shrugged it off as scarcely worthy of comment.

Being here made it different . . . not that their chances
were any greater, but that it was their own problem, and
it had to be dealt with. He studied what chances they
might have. First they could hope they were not discovered, and then, being discovered, they could fight with
the idea of taking as many Apaches with them as possible.

Two men at the canyon mouth could do a job of
standing off any attack for a while, and he himself could
keep them from getting to the canyon rim for a while.
They would get around behind him eventually, and then
if he was still alive he would retreat to the canyon. After
that they would defend the house as long as they could.

He chuckled grimly, remembering Shoyer. The man-
hunter had bought himself a basket of trouble this time,
and if he got out of here alive he would be lucky.

All was quiet below. The Indians had started a fire

and were killing one of their spare horses. Nothing an Apache liked better than horse meat except mule meat . . . no Apache, he remembered irrelevantly, would eat fish.

Taggart lit his cigarette and stuck the match into the sand. He got out several cartridges and placed them in a neat row on a flat rock. They looked good there, ready for business. He put the Winchester down and sat back, watching the Indians moving about the fire, near the spring.

Thoughts of the women went through his mind. That Consuelo was a fine figure of a woman. Give a man a time in bed, but for staying quality, day in and day out living, she wouldn't hold a candle to Miriam Stark.

He thought of the strange feeling that had risen within him when he sat his horse in the darkness outside the canyon, knowing there was someone near, even knowing that someone was a woman and desirable. It made no sense, but there it was. He had known.

One of the Apaches was looking up the slope. He had a feeling, that warrior did . . . he had him a hunch. Maybe Taggart's attention had drawn their attention. He waited, watching without looking directly at them.

The Apache had stepped out from the rest now and was looking up the mountain. Taggart knew he could not be seen . . . the broken slabs of rock, the clusters of prickly pear, these were a perfect cover. Even if they caught a glimpse of him they might think it was just part of the prickly pear or the rock. But the attention of the Indian worried him.

Suddenly the Apache stepped out from the others and started up the slope, walking slowly, studying the ground occasionally, but coming right on. Taggart drew deep on his cigarette and squinted at the Indian. The wind was from the Indians and toward him, so he had not been worried about them smelling the smoke.

"You, anyway," he said, to himself, "you keep coming and I'll nail your hide to the mast. You I'll take with me."

He was thinking his bullet home, knowing where he would put it, how he would inhale, exhale slowly and then squeeze off his shot . . . and there would be a dead

Indian at the end of that shot. At that distance and with that target he would not, could not miss.

The Apache drew nearer. He was no more than eighty yards away now and he had paused. He was short and stocky, and Taggart could see his face clearly . . . broad at the cheekbones.

Taggart rubbed his cigarette out in the sand. He took up the rifle and balanced it in his hands, sighting briefly down the barrel at the middle of the Indian's chest. Then he lowered the Winchester and waited.

The Apache was looking up the slope and Taggart could see the glint of his eyes. And then there was a call from down the slope, and the warrior turned and went back down the hill. Taggart lowered his rifle and leaned it against the rock nearest his hand.

It was very hot.

Within the canyon there was no sound. The bare rock walls left narrow strips of shadow at their foot, and the rivulet of water had long ceased to run. The noon held still under the Arizona sun, breathless with the moment. Cicadas sang, a shrill accompaniment to the heat.

Miriam came to the door and brushed the hair back from her eyes. She looked down the canyon toward the mouth, but there was no sound. Adam and Pete Shoyer had gone there, and they would be waiting in the rocks near the canyon's opening, while according to Adam, Swante Taggart was somewhere on the mountainside above the canyon's rim.

"No need to worry," Adam had said. "There's a man who'll get along if anyone will."

Yet she did worry. He was up there alone, beyond their sight, and by now he would be growing hungry. That he had visited Adam earlier Miriam guessed, but Adam had made no comment.

An hour dragged slowly by, and then another. The Apaches seemed in no hurry to leave. Most of them rested in the sparse shade of brush or rocks near Mud Spring, while a few prowled restlessly among the hills, mostly toward Rockinstraw and Redmond Mountain.

Pete Shoyer came back to the house, a heavy, unwashed man as seen by daylight. He grinned widely at Miriam. "Hot down there," he said.

"Will they find us?"

Consuelo came to hear his reply, and Shoyer looked past Miriam at the Mexican girl. "You never know about 'Paches. The way I figure, they know I'm somewhere around."

He stood at the door and ate the plate of beans and *chia* that Consuelo brought him, his eyes continually straying down canyon.

Suddenly he chuckled. "That there Taggart . . . he sure won't try runnin', with those 'Paches out there. They'd have him tied to a cactus in no time."

"Mr. Taggart," Miriam replied quietly, "sees no reason why he should run. I doubt if you need worry about it. When this is over, if any of us are alive, he will be here."

Shoyer grinned insinuatingly. "You set store by him, looks to me. It sure looks to me."

"Not particularly," Miriam replied stiffly, "only I'm sure Mr. Taggart is a good man. He is not a criminal. He is not a murderer. Those men were encroaching on his land and they began the fight."

"Lady," Shoyer protested, "I ain't the judge. I only hunt him down and make an arrest."

"Or kill him . . . and all for money!"

Shoyer was not disturbed. "Don't give me that. I've had all that stuff shoved at me before this, an' it's just the way I make a livin'. Some folks work at one thing, some work at another. I work at what I'm best at."

"Why don't you forget Mr. Taggart?" Miriam asked. "When this is over, just ride on?"

He chuckled. "Lady, you really do go for that gent. You really do. Now, the way I'd figured," he glanced at Consuelo, "it was this other lady who went for him. Seemed to me that was a goin' thing."

"You're being rude."

Shoyer was not disturbed. "Maybe . . . that's the way I see it. How about it, Mex?"

Consuelo drew herself up. "I am married woman."

Shoyer shrugged. "Wouldn't be the first. Good-lookin' man, that Taggart. Now me . . . women folks never made no fuss about me. On'y when I had money. So I pull Taggart in, I have money."

He finished his plate and licked his lips off carefully, then rubbed his palms on the front of his trousers and accepted the coffee. He had taken the first swallow when they heard the shot.

It came from down canyon. It was sharp and clear, and left an echoing report that racketed against the rock walls.

Pete Shoyer threw down the cup and, rifle in hand, sprinted for the canyon mouth.

Miriam reached inside the door and took up her rifle.

Chapter 9

Swante Taggart had seen it coming. He had seen it happen.

It was the same Apache who had started up the slope. He had been called from the spring by a beckoning Indian, and had started back when something arrested his attention in the direction of the canyon mouth. Taggart saw the warrior stop, and for several minutes the Indian stood very still. Then, ever so carefully, he began to move toward the spot where the canyon emerged upon the desert.

Taggart, sure the Apache had seen some movement there and was stalking whoever was on guard there, lifted his rifle. He took careful aim, took up the slack on his trigger, then held his slack and waited. If that Apache started to lift his rifle Taggart would fire. The distance was now well over two hundred yards, but Taggart had no doubt of his shot.

Another shot came first.

The Apache made the slightest move upward with the rifle, then even as Taggart was about to squeeze off his shot the Indian buckled at the knees and pitched forward on his face, the echo hanging in the still air.

For an instant, Taggart believed he himself had shot.

The dust-brown body of the Apache lay in plain sight, sprawled on a clump of prickly pear, the sun gleaming redly on the blood-splashed leaves.

Nothing else moved.

Taggart shifted his attention to the group around Mud Springs . . . but there was no group! There was nobody at all. There were only the horses and the slow, thin spiral of the rising smoke from the campfire.

Sweat trickled down his cheek. Taggart eased his tension on the trigger and, keeping his eyes on the slope, dug out the makings. The sun glinted from a rifle barrel . . . something was moving down there, but Taggart held his fire. No use to let them know what happened until necessary.

The dead Indian lay where he had fallen, nailed with the first shot.

Overhead a buzzard sailed in the blue-brassy sky, and in the far distance over the Four Peaks a few white clouds hung still in the sky. His foot was cramped and he shifted position.

No chance to avoid the fight now . . . they were in for it. Only there was nothing to shoot at. Nothing to do but wait. Down below they would be ready. Stark and Shoyer would be at the canyon mouth, the girls at the house, and he was here, high on the slope of the mountain with the canyon falling off on his right hand.

Whatever the dead Indian had seen or believed he saw had not been communicated to the others. The Apaches did not know what had happened, and right now they would be starting to move, to investigate.

The trouble was, the visibility was not good enough. The air was sharp and clear, but the slope was dotted with brush, and there was brush in the hollow near the canyon mouth. Swante Taggart turned slowly and studied the mountain above and around him. A man never took anything for granted in this country if he wanted to keep his hair.

Suddenly he realized he was holding an unlit cigarette in his teeth, and he struck a match with his left hand and lifted it to the cigarette. Just then an Apache came out of the juniper below him and started across the slope. He had worked his way up the slope and was not over fifty yards away, and if he reached the canyon at that level he could look down upon the buildings.

Taggart fired the rifle with one hand, lifting it and squeezing off the shot.

The Indian stumbled, but he did not go down. Like a wounded cat the Apache wheeled, and when he started to lift his rifle Taggart shot into his body, aiming from the shoulder this time. The Indian took a short quick step up the slope, and then went down to his hands and knees.

Rifle ready, Taggart watched him there. He could see the man was bleeding, so he held his fire. A wounded Apache was doubly dangerous, but there was no use wasting fire if the man was dead.

The Indian started to get up, then slumped to the ground again.

And over the wide slope of the mountain there was no further sound, no movement.

Taggart shifted position, working his way through the brush and farther up the mountain. When he had found a good spot he settled down to wait.

Nothing happened. The sunlight was hot upon the hill's broad face. A bee buzzed around some sage nearby. Overhead a bird lit in a mesquite tree that grew where water had run down the mountainside. The sky was an empty silence, and below the desert and mountains lay still. Here and there rocks were acquiring shadows, but the sun was still high. A lizard stirred among some flat rocks. Taggart mopped the sweat from his brow and squinted his eyes against the sun.

They were out there. Not one of them, but at least two dozen . . . if his first count had been right, at least twenty-eight.

Two warriors had been slain, and as yet they had not seen any enemy. This was Apache work turned against Apaches. But Swante Taggart knew well enough that the odds were all against them. At this kind of fighting the Apache was clearly the greatest of them all, perhaps the greatest guerilla fighter the world had ever seen.

Only Taggart had learned from them, and so had Shoyer. Grimly, he suddenly realized he was pleased that Pete Shoyer had found him. Whatever else he was, the man-hunter was a first-class fighting man.

A slow hour passed. Nothing stirred. The Apache horses stood in the wash near Mud Springs, clearly visible. Suddenly, he was aware that there were now fewer horses than there had been. One by one they were being spirited away.

Yard by yard he searched the terrain. From the far slope of Rockinstraw he worked his eyes back and forth along the slope, and on down to Mud Springs. Then he searched around him and above him. When he looked toward the horses again, another was gone.

A line-back dun stood near some brush at the edge of the wash, and he set himself to watching that horse. He sighted his rifle at the horse, then eased it down and took a quick look around. Then he waited.

He had been looking at the object for several minutes before he realized that it was a bush that had not been there a few minutes before. While he watched he saw the bush inch closer to the dun.

Lifting his rifle he cradled it in his hands, waited an instant, and then squeezed off his shot. It was an easy shot, and the Indian sprang forward in a lunge, his leg buckling under him. Even so he grabbed the dun and jerked him back into the brush before Taggart could get off another shot.

Instantly, Taggart was moving, working his way up hill, drawing closer to a place where he could, if it became necessary, get back into the canyon of the chapel. There had been no more firing from the canyon mouth.

The sun declined a little, the shadows pushed out toward the east, and nothing happened. He glanced toward the place where the first Apache had fallen across the prickly pear. The body was gone, slipped away while he was busy with the other. It was the Indian custom to remove their dead whenever possible.

It must be that the Apaches did not know of the canyon of the chapel, for had they known the attack would have begun before this. At this moment they were undoubtedly scouting the area trying to find out where their enemy was and how many there were.

The first shot from the canyon opening and then the other from up the slope evidently had them puzzled. Obviously they had been trailing Shoyer, and probably they did not know now whether they fought one man or more than one.

This gave Taggart an idea. Picking up a small rock, he shied it into a clump of brush some distance away, throwing it into the leafy top of the brush where the falling stone would rustle. A few minutes later he tossed one into a small gravel slide farther south along the slope. A few bits of gravel rattled over stones and were still. If it did nothing else, it would puzzle them and make them wary, and the hour was already well along. But Apaches were wary of night fighting, and they might not attack until daybreak. The stretching shadows would offer even more cover for attackers.

Taggart fed a couple of cartridges into his Winchester, and searched the terrain around him. His present position bottled him close against the edge of the canyon, with thick brush and rocks all around. At the very edge of the brush the field of vision was good, but he had to move to look up slope, and that bothered him. To move was to expose himself to danger, and so far he had made his moves with the greatest care and under almost perfect concealment. The stillness, too, was disturbing.

Two Apaches dead, one wounded, out of two dozen or more. Swante Taggart knew they had been lucky in taking first blood from the Indians, but he also knew what that number of Apaches could do, and they could not expect to be so lucky from this time forward.

There were two alternatives. Stay and fight it out, or try to make a run for it. Either meant risk, either meant the odds would all be against survival. Nobody outside knew they were here, nobody was in a way to discover their presence and send relief, so whatever was done they must do themselves.

The shadows were growing longer. The sun cast its final red lances into the sky, and the clouds lined themselves with gold. With darkness the Apaches might withdraw to their camp near Mud Spring . . . but they might not.

Miriam had mentioned a back way out to which she could bring a horse, a route that led over the mountains and down toward Globe. He thought about that now.

Taggart got to his knees and worked his way around behind a cedar that clung to the canyon's rim. From there he studied the situation and liked none of it. Yet the time had come to get back into the canyon . . . if he intended to. Of course, he need not return at all. He could take his own chances, moving at night, hiding by day. His strength was built up again, and he knew what he could stand. It was no distance to Globe.

He crouched, then ran in a crouching run for a clump of boulders ahead of him. He was almost there when an Apache raised up from the rocks and aimed a rifle at his chest, and another one started over the rocks toward him. He fired his rifle from the hip, but in the instant before he fired the Indian seemed to be struck from behind and he fell face forward, sliding down the rocks, and the report of a rifle thudded hard at close range.

The other Apache was coming and Taggart jammed him in the belly with the muzzle, then jerked it up under the Apache's chin. The Indian staggered back, clawing and gasping, and Taggart hit him a wicked butt stroke with his rifle, knocking him sprawling. From somewhere behind him a shot *whiffed* by his ears, and at the same moment a rifle ahead of him opened fire on the brush behind him.

Ducking and running, he made toward that covering fire. It was Miriam. She was standing in a notch where two boulders left a slit between them and she was handling her rifle like a veteran.

For a moment then, as he leaped and lit rolling, there flashed into his mind a picture of her there that reminded him of his mother, of his aunt . . . of all the pioneer women who had come west with their men. He sat up, and got slowly to his feet, shaken by the tumble he had taken.

She was perfectly calm. Her cheeks were a little whiter and there was a wisp of red-brown hair hanging over her cheekbone. He brushed himself off, thinking about her as she stood there. This was a woman fit to mother a race of men . . . completely and entirely a woman, and with courage and coolness that won his amazed respect.

"Are you all right?"

He chuckled. "Now is that a fit question to be asking a man? I should be asking you."

They looked at each other, and then they both laughed. As one person, they turned to study the slope below and around them, but there was nothing in sight. An evening breeze moved over the slope with gentle fingers and rustled the dry leaves, but there was no other sound. Whatever Apaches were out there were lying quiet.

"You're like the ironwood," she said suddenly. "You were bred for this country."

Then they were silent. The last gold was fading from the rims of the distant clouds. The Four Peaks loomed somber in the far distance, and Rockinstraw bulked hugely against the sky.

Nothing stirred out there, and he lowered his rifle to wipe away the dust from the mechanism, and to check his guns. He fed a couple of shells into the Winchester, and waited. They could go . . . he was sure the Indians had drawn back for the moment, but neither was disposed to leave.

"I like the desert plants," she said suddenly. "They hold themselves back . . . so many of them have no leaves, no flowers, and then there is a rain and they leaf out and blossom. It's as if they knew they needed just that much rain to make a go of it, and when they have it they blossom and seed, and then they retire within themselves very quickly."

"In the California deserts, along the washes," he said, "they have smoke trees . . . they call them that because at a distance they look like the smoke of a campfire . . . and the only way their seeds can be made to sprout is after they have been battered and bruised and worn down by being carried down a rocky wash, because they need the occasional water to grow."

The flat top of Rockinstraw now had a crest of dull red from the fading sun. Somewhere a quail called into the night, trying its stillness for a response. A nighthawk flipped and dived overhead, and a lone star hung like a lantern in the blue-black sky.

"We'd better go," he said, but still they did not move.

The desert was quiet . . . only the faint wind rustled among the juniper, humming a little, and a stone rattled in a rocky crevice somewhere beyond their range of sight.

"I like this," she said. "I'd really never want to live anywhere else. Not any more, I wouldn't."

"If you look for them," Taggart said, "and know them when you see them, there are old trails . . . they must be thousands of years old, for even the rocks in the trail are covered with desert varnish from the years of exposure to the sun. I've followed some of them for miles.

"Sometimes when a man is right on top one of those trails he can't see it unless he has a feeling for them, but from across a canyon they're visible."

"Where do they go?"

"Some of them to water, and some to piñon groves, and some just go on and on. I heard once they went clear to the Pacific coast."

"What are you going to do now?"

"You mean what am I going to do about Shoyer?"

"After that."

He chuckled. "Don't seem to me like I'd better start rounding up my cattle until I'm sure I'll have a brand for them. If Shoyer has his way I may do nothing from here on. He's a mighty persuasive man with a gun."

"I hate him!"

Taggart took her by the arm. "Unless we want to fall down that path instead of walk, we'd better light out."

They started, and descended into the blackness and coolness of the canyon. The path was a mere eyebrow of trail, switching over and back along the steep face, part of it along natural fractures, and part apparently cut from the wall.

As they neared the pool they could hear the trickle of falling water, and then Adam Stark stepped from the shadow near the chapel and said, "I was getting worried."

"Anybody hurt?" Taggart asked.

"We were lucky. Did you score?"

"One gone, one hurt in this last scuffle. The same earlier."

"The one you hit with the butt is dead, I think."

"Maybe. Anyway, that's at least three down, maybe four."

They paused at the door and waited for Shoyer, who was coming up the canyon. "Don't anybody go down there without me," Shoyer said when he was near. "I rigged a trip wire to a shot gun. Slightest touch and she's gone. I figured we'd have to do some talking."

"I think we should pull out," Taggart said, "all of us."

Chapter 10

The firelight made shadow play upon the wall as they gathered in the room. Consuelo lighted a candle to give a better light and Adam sat down abruptly.

There was no question in any of their minds as to what must be done, nor that it must be done immediately. There were two dozen Apaches out there, and when daylight came all escape would be cut off. Remaining where they were was out of the question, for once the Apaches reached the edges of the canyon the defenders would be pinned down to the buildings, and the roofs could be burned.

To east, west, and north it was a great distance to any place where help or safety might be found, and if escape was to be made it must be toward the south, toward Globe. The quickest and easiest route lay past Mud Springs and over to Pinal Creek where the Apaches had camped, or else around Rockinstraw Mountain. The only alternative was the escape route suggested by Miriam to Taggart.

At best they would have but a few hours' start, with about twenty miles to go if they took that roundabout route.

"Pack food for four days," Taggart said. "I'll get the horses."

"*Four* days!" Shoyer exclaimed. "If we aren't in Globe by tomorrow night we'll be dead, or wishing we were."

"Four days," Taggart repeated, "or even five. We might have to hole up somewhere, and if we hide out we'll need the grub."

"Five mounts and a pack horse," Shoyer said. "Do you have that many?" he asked of Stark.

"Taggart has his own horse, but we'll need six pack horses. And we have that many."

Outside the door Taggart paused to let his eyes adjust to the darkness. It was true that Apaches rarely attacked by night, for they believed the soul of a warrior killed in darkness must wander forever, lost in the vast emptiness of a night without stars. But Swante Taggart was not inclined to be killed by the one Apache who might be willing to take a chance.

Swiftly he saddled his own horse and arranged the little pack behind the saddle, gathering his few belongings and putting his extra shells in his pockets. He checked the rifle taken from the Apache he had killed on the trail and added a couple of shells, then shoved it into the boot on his own saddle. His rifle he kept in his hands.

Several times he stopped to listen, but there was no sound. He gathered the horses and mules and led them down to the stable, where he began saddling up. Pete Shoyer came out to join him and they worked in silence, then Pete went up the canyon to fill their canteens.

Suddenly there was a movement behind Taggart and he turned swiftly, grabbing at the dark figure. It was a woman . . . Consuelo.

"You are strong, Señor."

He let go of her arms. "You ought to be careful, slipping up on a man thataway."

"Swante Taggart," she stepped closer to him, "I want to go with you. Take me now . . . take me away."

"You're Stark's woman."

"He will be kill. With him the Apaches get me, but you will escape. I know it."

"You're a lot of woman," Taggart replied, "but I'm taking no man's wife."

She grasped his arm. "There is gold! Adam will bring the gold. Take it, and take me. You can go faster and you will escape. Adam will be dead. I know he will be dead. There is no chance for him because he is not strong."

"Ma'am," Taggart spoke softly, "you aren't thinking right. You're excited and you're scared, but you just slow down and think about this. Take it from me, you've got the best man you're likely to find, and you run off from him and you'll end up in a worse jack-pot than anybody. You just stand by Adam and you'll come out all right."

"You are fool! You can escape. Why you stay? You owe these people nothing! And Pete Shoyer will kill you!" She paused. "Why not take the gold? He says he wants it for me, but he will die, and I want to live."

Swante Taggart had nothing to say. He knew what it meant to be frightened, for he had seen frightened people before this, and this girl was not afraid of shadows. She had been with Apaches and knew what to expect. Before she had been a child, and the Apaches loved children . . . but now she was a woman and she had witnessed what happened to women in the hands of Apaches.

She was afraid, desperately afraid, and having no confidence in Stark, she was grasping at anything to get away.

Shoyer came up in the darkness but Consuelo had gone, slipping away as silently as she had come. "Look," Shoyer said, "you make one try at gettin' away and I'll pay no mind to taking a prisoner back when a head will do as well."

Taggart turned away, disgusted. "Oh, shut up!" he said.

Stark was coming from behind the house carrying a sack. It was small, but very heavy. He lifted it to a sack on one of the pack saddles, and Shoyer watched him. When he had gone Shoyer went to the mule and hefted the sack. "Well, what d' you know?" he said softly.

Stark came out with another sack and loaded it on the other side, and returned to the cache behind the house.

"Six pack mules, and five of them packing gold. I'd say he'd struck it rich now, wouldn't you?"

"I'd also say," Taggart answered, "that it's none of our affair."

Miriam came from the house, bringing her few belongings, and Consuelo followed. Taggart had completed the saddling of the horses and he turned to, helping Stark load his gold.

Reluctantly, they faced the necessity for moving. Now that the time had come they hesitated, for once outside the canyon all security was gone. It was Adam Stark who led off, followed by Shoyer and Consuelo, then the pack mules, and Taggart brought up the rear with Miriam.

No such cavalcade can move without sound, and Swante Taggart, riding the drag of the small mule train, expected sound. Yet there was remarkably little. The black walls of the canyon soared above them, drawing closer like the closing jaws of some great beast, and the tiny strip of visible sky grew narrower with each step, and the visible stars were fewer.

Leather creaked, hoofs clicked on stone, and occasionally a man sighed or grunted, but there was no other sound. Taggart put a hand to his brow and found himself sweating despite the night's clear coolness. He was prepared to hear the sudden blasting of rifles at any moment, but there was nothing.

Suddenly the trail grew steeper, and they mounted ever higher until they appeared about to come out at the rim of the canyon. Then they turned downward again into the abysmal blackness of the gorge.

When at last they started up once more, they mounted to the canyon rim, with the mountain looming ahead to their right. They halted there in the starlight and Stark walked his mount back along the train to be sure all were present.

"It's southeast from here," he said, "for about a half mile, and then south along the foot of the cliff. We're up high now, only a few hundred feet lower than the peak of Rockinstraw, and further along we'll have to go up the cliff to hit the trail that will take us into the Basin. If we're all right at that point we've got a chance."

There was no question of making speed. To keep moving and keep together was all they could expect. They all sat their horses with care, prepared for the unexpected.

Taggart kept looking back, although he could see nothing but the blackness. His rifle was across the saddle in front of him.

Miriam dropped back beside him. "Do we have a chance?"

"Sure."

"Adam isn't sure about this trail, and he might stray. He's worried himself, but he's good at such things, and the man who told us of it gave us a pretty good description. Adam was up this way once, and followed it along for some distance."

"Things shape up mighty different at night. Landmarks don't look the same . . . nothing does."

Drawn together by the companionship of night travel they rode in silence, each feeling the comfort of the other's presence. But Swante Taggart was worried too. Her presence was pleasant but it was disturbing, and this was a time when he dare not be disturbed. He listened, and once he thought he heard a faint sound off in the night, but he did not hear it again.

After a long time they halted again. Several minutes passed and there was no movement, and just when Taggart had decided to go forward to see what had happened, Shoyer came back.

"Stark went on ahead to scout the trail. He's afraid we missed a turn back there somewhere."

"Better to be sure."

Taggart sat silent, wondering what the other man was thinking. Each of them needed the other now, so each felt safe from the other, unworried about a sudden shot from the darkness. Or was it that way?

"If we should be separated," Shoyer said suddenly, "you go your way. You leave me alone and I'll leave you alone," and he went ahead again.

Taggart sat still, staring after Shoyer. "Now what did he mean by that?" he demanded.

"Maybe he has decided to relent and let you go."

"No." Taggart felt positive about that. "It isn't like him. He wouldn't let me go. Not unless he found something better."

The mules started and they followed after, moving slowly through the darkness. Several times they halted briefly, and twice they changed direction in the darkness. Taggart looked at the stars and swore, and then he glanced at the bulk of the cliff on their right.

He drew up sharply as the idea hit him, but at first it seemed impossible. Then he said to Miriam, "Wait here!" and rode swiftly forward.

The mules were strung out far too much, and when he reached the head of the train, the mule there was calmly chewing at a clump of sage and there was no one anywhere near.

"Stark?" he called softly into the night, but the night gave back no answer. He tried it again, just a little louder, and still there was no reply.

He called Shoyer's name then, and Consuelo's, but no answer came. Turning swiftly, suddenly frightened for Miriam, he rode back.

She sat her saddle waiting. "What is it, Swante?" she asked. "What's wrong?"

It was the first time she had used his first name. He realized that on a level of consciousness somewhere above and beyond the immediate problem.

"We're alone," he said, "they're gone."

"Gone?"

The word had no meaning to her in that moment. They could not be gone. It was impossible.

"I don't understand. Who is gone?"

"All of them . . . we're alone."

She was silent for a moment. "I heard you call . . . but where could they go? Why would they go?"

He was not listening, he was thinking. There was no sound in the night except the crunch of a mule's jaws as it munched on some of the brush along the trail.

It was completely dark, the trail was strange to them all, and that Apaches were around was unlikely, yet the three other riders had dropped from sight as if they had fallen off the edge of the world.

To look for tracks in this darkness was beyond reason, and to make a light would be foolhardy.

"Miriam," he said quietly, "we're in trouble."

Chapter 11

At best they had come no more than eight or nine miles from the Apache *rancheria* at Mud Springs. Their route had been difficult, a trail strange to them, with many brief halts. To wander about now searching for tracks would be to destroy whatever trail might have been left. On the other hand, the three might have gone on ahead for some reason and would soon return . . . in fact, they might believe Taggart and the mules were following.

Yet following where? Before them all lay in darkness, and no clearly defined trail could be seen.

"What will we do?" Miriam asked. "Adam would not just go off and leave us."

"We'll wait," Taggart replied.

Every minute of travel was a minute added to their lives, but in the darkness they might get into a cul-de-sac from which no escape was possible.

Bunching the mules together took only a few minutes, but even in the darkness he detected something was wrong. Working around among the mules he discovered one was missing. It was one of the mules carrying gold.

"I don't like it," he said in a low tone. "It isn't just them now . . . there must be around twenty thousand dollars on that mule."

Miriam dismounted and stood close to him in the silence as they strained their ears for some sound, some evidence that the others were not far off.

Here among the high peaks it was cool. Now a late moon rose, and the bare rocks took on a weird effect in the pale light. Below and all around them there were pines, and a wind moved among them, where the sound of its humming seemed like faint music.

Leaving Miriam on watch with the mules, Taggart went ahead, keeping to one side of the direct line they had followed, and searching ahead, but there was nothing.

To go or to stay? Taggart paused on the mountainside, pondering. To remain here long was to ask for death. He made his decision suddenly. They must go on. They must find some place where the mules could be hidden. They had food, and with luck they could remain in hiding for days.

He walked back to Miriam. "Mount up," he said, "we're going on."

She was not the sort to protest, to demand explanations, or to waste time in needless discussion or suggested alternatives. It was enough that Taggart had decided, and she trusted that decision.

They moved out with Taggart in the lead and Miriam close behind, only this time the mules were on a lead rope.

The moonlight gave them some visibility. Taggart led cautiously, searching for some sign of the others, and at the same time watching for a place where they could hole up for a few hours, and give themselves time to make a quick survey of the area, in the hope of finding out what had happened to Adam Stark and the others.

The trail suddenly started up the cliff. It went twenty yards ahead, switched back for twice that distance, and then went forward again. Although the cliff was no more than five hundred feet up, it took them nearly an hour to negotiate the climb. From the condition of the trail Taggart was sure nobody had been over it before them. Twice he was forced to dismount and shift slabs of rock from the trail, fallen there long ago.

At the summit they drew up to catch their wind. Around them stretched a vast and unbelievable moonscape of peaks and shoulders and serrated ridges, bathed in pale moonlight cut by canyons of darkness, and vast gulfs that were only black. It was an eerie place, and the wind hummed weirdly among the scattered pines.

A few hundred yards farther on Taggart saw a flat-topped mesa, low and broad, rising above the plateau they had reached. They were no higher than Rockinstraw, which he could see off to the northwest. Pushing on, he looked toward the low mesa and turned off toward it. He left Miriam, and went on ahead and searched until he found a way to the top.

The mesa was fifteen or twenty acres in extent, and at one side of it was a low place, deep enough to allow concealment for the pack train. There a pool of water had gathered from the recent rain, covering perhaps half an acre, but from what he could see, only a few inches deep.

Leading the pack train to the top, Taggart concealed them in the small basin. Then he sat with Miriam at the edge of the mesa, overlooking the country. The air was very cool, the sky held only a few scattered clouds, and below them all was darkness except for the peaks and ridges which stood out of the blackness like islands in a dark sea. Above them, all was sky. They were lost here, as if on another world.

Miriam spoke suddenly. "Pete Shoyer has killed men for a few hundred dollars of reward money. Wouldn't such a man kill for what gold was on one of those mules?"

Swante Taggart drew a long breath. It was this he had been considering. There were men he knew who would not kill except in the name of the law . . . but there were others who would. The distinction between the peace officers of the time and the outlaw was either sharply drawn or it was scarcely drawn at all.

"Consuelo spoke to me," he said, "so maybe she spoke to Shoyer next. She's a mighty scared girl, Miriam. She has no faith whatever in Adam's ability to protect her. She wanted me to take her away."

"What about Adam?"

"That's what worries me."

He got to his feet. "I've got to leave you here alone, and whatever you hear, whatever you see, whatever you may think, you've got to stay right here. I've got to be sure you're here . . . and I don't think you'll ever be found here. But stay below the rim, stay out of sight."

"How long is it until daybreak?"

He glanced at the stars. "We've an hour at least, maybe close to two hours. At this altitude, being on top of everything around, it will come sooner for us than down below, but I've got to go down there and take a look. If anything's happened to Adam, I'll find him."

"All right," she said quietly.

He tightened the cinch on his saddle and stepped into

the leather. "And Miriam, keep your eyes open and keep your rifle close. It isn't only the Apaches you have to worry about now. There' Shoyer."

"You think he will com ack?"

"Maybe."

"A man who would kill for one mule-load of gold might not hesitate to kill for half a dozen . . . is that what you mean?"

"Adam isn't dead. I'm sure of that. No shot was fired, and there was no sound of fighting up ahead, no action at all that we could hear. I'm sure he is not dead."

Although he said that, he was thinking that a knife could be silent, a blade would make no sound.

Would Consuelo want Adam killed? He doubted it, but in her panic of fear . . . No, he would not believe it. Shoyer might kill, but not Consuelo. She would not kill Adam herself, nor want him killed.

But the question about Pete Shoyer worried Taggart. He had known such men before, and most of them were utterly ruthless in killing anyone suspected of crime, yet were often curiously reluctant to kill for any other reason. Pete Shoyer had the name of being a driving and relentless man, but so far as Taggart had heard there were no killings against him except those involved in the capture of criminals or wanted men. But now . . . ?

Miriam came and stood beside his horse, clinging to his hand. "Swante . . . come back."

"I will."

He pressed her hand, and then rode away, taking his horse down the steep trail to the plateau and along it to the trail up which they had come. He was more cautious now. Instinctively he was wary of a trail over which he had once come, and it was not his way to return by the same route, where an enemy might be lying in wait. At the moment, though, there was no alternative . . . he knew of no other trail, nor had he time to search for one in the darkness.

But he was aware that he rode into a double danger. In his own mind he was sure that Pete Shoyer had in some way put Adam Stark out of the running. And if Pete Shoyer had gone off the rails for a woman and a mule-load of gold, it would be like him to come back for the rest. Yet what had he said?

"If we should be separated you go your way. You leave me alone and I'll leave you alone."

His statement to Taggart had sounded like a declaration of peace between them . . . which meant that Taggart was free of pursuit, that he could go his own way. All he had to do was leave Shoyer alone.

Looked at from the present situation, it appeared that Pete Shoyer had already made his plans, had reached some agreement with Consuelo, and that even now they were moving somewhere down the dark canyons.

Dawn came slowly. At first it was only a suggestion of gray, then an infiltration of pale yellow, and a fading of stars. Swante Taggart sat hunched in the saddle for the air was chill, and he watched the eastern light catch the first distant peaks. Concealed among some trees, he waited and listened. There was little he could do until the light grew, but he might hear something.

He felt edgy and strange, not liking the situation, knowing they should be running for Globe and not waiting here. He was not concerned with Shoyer . . . the man could handle his own problems. Adam Stark was something else, for he was a man too good to waste. Even now he might be a prisoner of the Apaches, or lying dead in a canyon. When the light grew he would make a search.

Taggart's eyes kept turning toward Rockinstraw, now miles away, looking for the first faint hint of smoke. There was nothing. But by this time, he was sure, something was happening over there.

Apaches were cautious, and they had been trapped the day before and would be even more wary now, so they would enter the canyon with great care. And care meant time, and it was time Taggart needed now.

Leaving Miriam alone worried him, although her position was as safe as could be found. She was not only concealed from sight, but was in an unlikely place for any searcher to look. She was much better off than he was himself, for even at this moment he might be under the eyes of an Apache. Or of Shoyer.

But if Shoyer decided to take the rest of the gold, he might well track them down and find Miriam alone, and such a man if he went lawless would be dangerous far beyond most outlaws.

Red now tinged the sawtoothed edges of the far hills and bled down the sides of peaks like glowing lava. Taggart warmed his hands by chafing them and then, rifle in hand, he walked his horse out on the trail.

It was a confusion of tracks, mule and horse tracks left from the night before. Working ahead, he found the place where their own tracks and those of the pack train vanished on the rocky surface of the shelf, but he could find no others. Going back along the trail with infinite caution, he searched for any tracks that deviated from the group, and from time to time he paused to search the country around him.

He was jumpy. Time was growing shorter, and he knew the Apaches would soon be on their trail. He rode keyed for action and the horse sensed it. Presently he was back where they had waited the night before, where the fact that the others were missing had first been discovered.

He turned in his saddle and looked toward the mesa where Miriam waited. It was high against the sky, stark and bare in its treeless outline, and there was no movement there, no sign of trouble or even of life. It stood black against the early morning sky, catching a little of the first light before the sun's rising.

He rode on, and suddenly saw a place where there was boot-torn ground at the trail's edge. There had been a struggle here, or perhaps a body had been dragged. It was difficult to tell, and nothing could be seen over the edge, for the cliff bulged out to form an overhang.

Taggart stood still, taking time to look around, feeling nervous as a cat. It had been a long time since he had been so edgy, so aware of danger. He touched his dry lips with his tongue and longed for a smoke, but even that was a danger.

Now he must find a way down that declivity. Unless he was very wrong, Adam Stark, alive or dead, lay at the bottom of it. From the height of the cliff—eighty feet or more—Taggart had few hopes, for no man could have fallen down there onto the jagged rocks below and lived.

He turned his horse and began the search for a trail.

On top of the mesa, Miriam moved among the mules, talking to them, touching them. It was too cold to sit still, and it would be some time before the sun warmed this chill basin. The flat top of the mesa was mostly covered by a thin soil, but around the pool it was only rock, a blue-black basaltic rock as cold as iron.

The mules and horses, after their march of the previous night, were content to drowse. Leaving them, rifle in hand, Miriam climbed to the rim of the little basin until she could see over the edge of the mesa.

Nothing.

Far off, the eastern sky was a pale lemon touched with scarlet.

Looking off into the morning, she knew she was in love and that she had never loved until now. So little had passed between them, so few words had been said, so little had been done. For such a bold man, Taggart seemed almost shy, and hesitated to so much as touch her, yet she knew what there was in him, and what was within herself. And now he was down there, away from her and in danger, searching the canyons.

Her own hiding place had been well chosen, for it seemed as if the flat top of the mesa would offer no shelter whatsoever, as unlikely a place as one could find. Nevertheless, there was no safe place short of Globe, and she had little faith in anything but a temporary security here.

Sunrise came suddenly. The sky was clear, the mountains lost their shadows, and they stood in pinks and reds, and the green of forest. Over her the sky stretched vast and lonely, incredibly enormous, incredibly blue. From below there was no sound at all. It was as though she were alone in the universe, as though no one lived but herself.

She was hungry, but she dared not build a fire, even if fuel had been available, and there was nothing here, not a stick nor a cow chip. Near the lip of the rock basin some grass grew, and Miriam pulled some of it for the mules. When she had an armful she dropped it before them. She went back for more without venturing beyond the basin itself, and this kept her occupied until the sun was well over the horizon. She succeeded in finding grass and sage enough to give all the stock a few mouthfuls.

For a long time she watched over the rim of the basin but saw nothing. No smoke, no dust of riders, simply nothing at all. She still had the feeling that she might be alone in the world.

And then, just short of noon, she saw a thin column of dust, which appeared above the trail in the direction from which they had come. Engrossed, she did not hear the slow movement behind her until too late. When she turned she looked into Pete Shoyer's gun muzzle.

"I never killed a woman," he said, "but the gold on those mules would make it mighty easy. Now you make trouble and I'll do just that."

He looked about. "Where's Taggart?"

"He's around." Miriam looked past Shoyer at Consuelo. "I didn't think it of you, Connie."

Consuelo's face was sullen. "I want to go away. I want to live. He will take me away."

"But not fast enough, I think." Then to Shoyer, "Why didn't you take what you had and keep going? Why must you come back for the rest of it?"

Shoyer was gathering up the tie-ropes of the mules. "Might as well go the whole hog," he said calmly. "If a man goes this route it should pay off."

"Now they'll be hunting you for the reward," Miriam replied.

He paused an instant, as if the idea had not occurred to him before. "They'll never know," he said then. "They don't know you folks are out here. They wouldn't believe you had this much gold. There's nobody to know."

"I'm here."

He looked at her. "I've been thinking of that."

"And there's Taggart as well as Adam. And there's Connie."

"Adam is out of it, and Taggart will be. As for Connie, she's with me."

Miriam looked at Consuelo. "Did you let him kill Adam? Did you?"

"He did not kill him. Adam fall. He backed up when

100

Pete came for him, and he fell off the edge of the cliff."

"However it happened," Miriam replied coolly, "you and Shoyer are responsible. You are not only thieves, you are murderers."

Pete Shoyer chuckled, but it was without humor. "Names don't hurt me. We'll be sitting in the Palace Hotel in 'Frisco living off the fat of the land. You call us what you will."

"He was good to you, Connie. Adam never hurt anyone who didn't ask for it. Like your friend Tom Sanifer."

Consuelo's head came up. "What you mean? Adam was 'fraid of Tom Sanifer."

"He was not, and it's time you knew it. Adam never liked men who bragged in front of women, or quarreled before them. He went down to the saloon in Bowie and called Sanifer, and Tom Sanifer was yellow. He would not fight."

"That's a lie!" Consuelo was staring at her. "It is not true!"

"It is, though. And then Tom Sanifer waited outside behind some barrels to kill Adam. Only he missed and Adam didn't. Tom Sanifer did not come back because he could not. He was dead."

"I do not believe that."

"Taggart knew it. He knew it all the time. He told me."

"It is a lie," Consuelo insisted stubbornly.

Miriam turned on Shoyer. "Tell her," she said. "You've heard of that fight."

"Sanifer was a loud-mouth," Shoyer agreed. "He had no sand. Nothing to him but flash . . . anybody could have killed him."

Consuelo was shaken but still stubborn. "I do not believe it," she said again.

Miriam searched her mind for something she could do to keep them here. "Taggart will come," she said, "and wherever you go he will follow."

"We ain't going any place," Shoyer said, "until we're sure. I've an idea your Taggart is going to be mighty glad he's free. He'll get out of the country while the getting is good. Him and me, we had an understanding to that effect."

Miriam turned away sharply. Not for a minute did she

believe in that understanding, yet if Shoyer was going to remain, then she must try to warn Swante Taggart before he returned.

How long had he been gone? It was only when she realized the hour that she was really worried. He had left well before daylight . . . it must have been about three or a little later. And it was now past noon. Where could he be?

And then she remembered the dust cloud, forgotten in the sudden arrival of Shoyer and Consuelo. There was no dust cloud now.

"What about the Apaches?" she asked Shoyer.

He considered the question and then said, "Taggart picked a good place, and I don't believe they'll find us here. We'll stay out the day and take off from here just after nightfall. At daybreak we'll be in Globe."

There was time then . . . time for Swante to return. Maybe he had found Adam. She could not believe Adam was dead, and would not believe it until she had seen his body.

Shoyer had taken her rifle, and there was nothing she could do but wait until Taggart returned and hope to find some way to warn him. It must be some way that Shoyer would not expect . . . but what?

She sat down, realizing that the first problem was not to give Pete Shoyer any idea as to her intentions. He did not know her, and she doubted that he had discussed her with Connie . . . there was too much else for them to talk about. So he might not expect trouble from her. She tried to consider what might be done, but nothing occurred to her that seemed either practical or possible.

But there was one thing she thought she could do, and must do, and that was to win Consuelo away from Shoyer.

The Mexican girl had unusual courage . . . Miriam had seen her stand unafraid in many cases of trouble and danger, yet because of her childhood experiences she had a wild, unreasoning fear of the Apaches. It was this, Miriam believed, that had made her desert Adam and try to escape. The very fact that they were here was evidence that she had gained little by the attempt.

As for Pete Shoyer, she knew little of such men, but

enough to know that for him the law had been a way of life, despite the fact that the way he had enforced the law had in itself often been lawless. She had seen men influenced by their own professed beliefs and habits of thinking. Shoyer, regardless of anything else, had acted for the law. And in the present circumstance this was now was a weakness, for some part of his mind must be given over to worry.

The first fear she hoped had been implanted by her suggestion that a reward would soon be offered for him, and that bounty-hunters would then be on his trail. To a man-hunter, knowing the forces arrayed against him better than any ordinary cowhand turned rustler, this idea could not but be disturbing.

Some sudden movement by Shoyer caught her eye. Then the man was absolutely still, listening. As she started to move, he lifted a hand to stop her, and she too listened.

Consuelo stood as if frozen. Better than any of them, she knew the sound they now heard. It was a sound of unshod hoofs upon stone. Then came a mutter of voices, Apache voices. It sounded as if they were arguing about something, but they passed on.

Pete Shoyer looked to Consuelo. "Did you get any of that?" he asked.

"I get all of it," Consuelo replied bitterly. "Some of them think we are near, and they are going to camp while they look for us."

Shoyer considered that. "They'll find us, then. No way they can miss, because sure as shootin' one of them will come up here to have a look around the country. That means we've got to make a fight for it."

"You took my rifle," Miriam said.

"If you need it, you'll get it back, but not until then."

Shoyer crawled to the lip of the basin and lay there. Whatever she might have done for Swante, Miriam knew she could do nothing now, for now she was fighting for her own life as well. Let this be settled first, and then they could fight things out among themselves.

As for Consuelo, she had gone out of one kind of trouble into a worse kind. They had all had their chance to escape, and had they continued without interruption they might now be near Globe, or even safely within the town. The action by Shoyer and Consuelo had cut off their escape, and now those two were themselves caught and faced with a fight for their lives. Only Taggart and Adam Stark were no longer with them.

"I wish Adam was here," Miriam said.

Consuelo's chin lifted, but she made no reply. Miriam was not planning to drop the subject. "You had a good man," she said. "He always kept us out of trouble, and you would have been in Globe now if you had not run off."

Consuelo turned her head and glanced at Miriam stonily from her magnificent black eyes. But she said nothing at all.

It was hot now, and the horses were restless. The mules, content with nothing to do, stood idly near the pool. No sound reached them now, and Miriam walked to the outer edge of the basin near the rim of the mesa. From here, except for a small ledge about fifty feet down, it was an almost sheer drop of six hundred feet. Off to the south, toward Globe, she thought she saw smoke rising, but it might be much nearer than the town.

Shoyer came to look out over the vast area below. Nothing moved. He walked back and stood beside Consuelo, pushing his hat back on his head.

"Don't you worry none," he said. "We'll get out of here, and all the gold with us."

Consuelo offered no comment, and he continued, "Once those 'Paches pull out, we can take the trail through the basin and down Nugget Wash. Be out of here in no time. You'll be eating supper in Globe."

"You think." There was an undertone of contempt in the comment which Shoyer did not notice. "If we had taken only one mule we would be in Globe now."

"And leave all the rest of it?" Shoyer chuckled. "Not on your life. That there is more money than most folks see in a lifetime, even to look at. Most banks don't carry that much, and this is ours, every bit of it."

"I do not care."

"You'll care. And don't you worry none about those 'Paches."

Miriam glanced around and saw her rifle lying against a boulder near the basin's rim. Turning, she walked slowly toward it. Just as she was about to pick it up, she raised her eyes.

An Apache rider sat on his horse at the edge of the mesa.

Chapter 12

It was well after daylight when Swante Taggart found Adam Stark. He discovered him by the broken brush above where he lay, and the broken limbs of a pine tree close under the rim of the trail.

Leaving his horse, Taggart struggled up through the rocks of an ancient lava flow that lay below the cliff. Here and there pines were growing up through the chunks of black lava as though through a pile of old burned-out clinkers. The marks of Stark's fall were clearly seen.

It was that broken brush and the broken branches where the body had fallen clear that allowed Taggart to hope, for he knew how little is required to break a man's fall and save his life. The breaking brush had slowed his tumble, and when he fell clear of the cliff face the branches he had broken in falling had deflected his fall. He had landed in the sand at the bottom of a dry waterfall where run-off water had come down from the mountain.

It took Taggart almost an hour before he got to Stark. Adam lay sprawled on the sand and there was a dark stain of blood in his hair and on the sand beneath him. Scrambling over the lava, Taggart knelt beside him and very gently turned him over. As he did so, Stark muttered and his eyes opened. For a moment he lay still, and then his eyes moved to Taggart.

"Lie quiet," Taggart said. "You had a bad fall."

He examined Stark swiftly, but could find nothing that seemed to be more than bad bruises and some abrasions. Just the same he was worried. Often he had seen a man able to get up from a bad fall when there had been something to break the fall; but there might be internal injuries.

In answer to the questioning look on Stark's face, he spoke to reassure him.

"Miriam is on top of the mountain with the mules. She's alone, and all the mules are there but one treasure mule. The place seems safe for a while."

"Connie?"

"Shoyer took her off somewhere. She's a badly frightened girl, Stark. How you ever got her up here in the first place is beyond me . . . as afraid of Apaches as she is."

Adam Stark struggled and sat up, Taggart watching him warily for some indication of injury. He allowed him to sit still, and as they waited he talked, partly to calm Stark and partly to let him know what the situation was.

"There's a lot of movement around," Taggart said, speaking softly. "We've got to get out of here and up on top of the mountain, and in broad daylight that's going to take time."

He had brought his canteen and now he handed it to Adam, who took a long drink, then put the cork back in place. "Let's get at it, then," Adam said.

Helped by Taggart he got to his feet, staggered a bit, and then slumped heavily. "Dizzy," he said. "Head going in circles."

Taggart let him rest while he searched around for his rifle. He found it, smashed beyond use. But he got at the magazine and shucked the .44's out of it and into his palm. There were fifteen shells. He passed them to Stark, who shoved them down in his pocket.

The rawhide thong had been in place and his pistol had not fallen from the holster. Stark removed the gun and spun the cylinder. "No damage there," he said. "But my head's aching like all get-out."

There was a cut along the side of his head almost at the crown, and where his jacket was torn there was a blood-stain. Later they would probably find plenty of damage, but Taggart's one idea was to get him moving before the shock wore off and he really began to feel his hurts.

Without further delay they moved out. Anxious as he was about Stark, Taggart could not keep his thoughts from Miriam. He was sure they would hear a shot if she were attacked, and there had been none; but they would have to travel at least a couple of miles, roundabout, to get where she was. He helped Stark over the rocks, and it was obvious that one leg was very stiff. He knew it was not broken, but it undoubtedly was badly bruised.

When they reached the horse, Taggart said to Stark, "You mount up. I'll walk." Despite Stark's protests, it was obvious they would travel faster with him in the saddle, and Taggart did not want to ride double . . . not yet.

Rifle in hand, Swante Taggart walked ahead of the horse. Carefully he worked his way along through the trees below the cliff, but now the cliff was less abrupt. Keeping under cover of the pines, pausing every few feet to study the country, they moved toward the point where Taggart had come down from above.

The sun was high now and Taggart was growing more and more worried. There was no hope of running now. Stark could make a fight of it from cover but, as he could tell from an occasional glance at the injured man, he must be feeling considerable pain.

By now the country would be alive with Apaches, and they were better than any hound on a scent, and far less easy to discourage. There was no evidence of Shoyer, but then, there was no reason for him to be down on this level of the mountain.

They paused under a huge, wind-racked pine, and Taggart studied their surroundings with care. Directly before them was a dim trail, visible only by the break in the vegetation, and it wound through the brush and back into a notch in the hills. Swante Taggart searched back through his memory but could remember nothing of such a trail, although it was likely this was a trail that came up along Wood Springs Wash. If so, it must cut around the end of the mountain where he had left Miriam.

Leaving the horse with Stark slumped in the saddle, Taggart went forward and scouted along the trail. To all appearances it had been long since anyone had used it. He turned back to where he had left Stark, and led the horse into the trail.

It was well covered. Here and there the pines stretched like a wall along either side, and occasionally a sycamore would reach long branches out to shade the trail. It was quiet here. It was too quiet.

He felt jumpy, and from time to time he paused, trying to steady himself, and keeping the rifle handy. Constantly he searched the country around for any movement. Stark was slumped in the saddle, obviously stifling his pain.

The vague trail now turned more to the northeast, and the mountain where Miriam waited was close by on their left. Finding what seemed a passable route, Taggart led the horse off the trail.

"Stark," he spoke softly, "from here on we're in trouble. Can you make it, or should I leave you here and come back for you?"

"I can make it." Stark stiffened himself in the saddle. "Just never knew a man could hurt in so many places. You lead on, Taggart. I'm with you."

Every step now was a danger, yet it seemed almost incredible, for all around them the country was so still in the warm sun. The air smelled fresh and clean of pines and sage, and there was no sound but an occasional stirring of wind.

Suddenly, a bird veered up sharply, and instantly Taggart was behind the bole of a tree, his Winchester ready. Stark had not moved for fear the saddle would creak, but his pistol was out and balanced easy in his hand.

After a moment, Taggart cat-footed it forward and paused. Not fifty feet away were three Apaches, but they faced in the opposite direction and were looking up the mountain ahead of them. This was the mountain where Miriam was and the Indians had seen something there. They moved away swiftly into the brush, climbing higher on the mountain.

"Looks like we got here just in time," Taggart said, and after another moment they went on.

From their actions, he decided there were few Apaches in this area. No doubt they had spread out to cover a wider range, and on sighting the pack train they would send up a smoke to bring the others to the fight. If his guess was right, that smoke would be going up soon.

The trees were thinning out, and before them loomed the bald mountain from which the mesa rose. Still all was quiet. Taggart led the horse beyond the last gathering of pines and into the sparse brush that straggled beyond the edge of the trees.

Three Apaches sat their horses some hundred yards away, and an Indian on foot was talking with them. While Taggart and Stark waited, another Indian came from the woods and joined them. Suddenly, from high on the mountain, there was a rifle shot.

The sound racketed down the rocks, and Taggart saw an Apache come tumbling down the slope, his body bringing up against a rock. The Indian struggled to pull himself erect, and then slumped back, losing hold on his rifle, which slid and rattled over the rocks.

Instantly, the others started forward, and Taggart lifted his rifle and took careful aim. It was an easy shot, but he made it with care, wanting to be sure of this at least of their enemies. He dropped the first Apache. Almost as if the rifle shot had been a magician's wand, the others vanished.

"Wait . . ." Taggart lifted a hand.

They stayed still, and nothing stirred.

"All right," Taggart said, "let's go!"

He left the brush on the run, keeping low, feeling that due to the lay of the ground, he had a chance of reaching the trail without being seen. But he had taken no more than a dozen steps before a bullet splattered against a rock near him and whined away through the hot afternoon. Stark was firing, and then from the rim of the mesa above there was a burst of rifle that startled Taggart.

Miriam was not alone! Pete Shoyer had come back, then.

They went up the slope, Stark on his horse and Taggart running, and they climbed up the mesa covered by rifle fire from the rim. He raced up and was a dozen steps over the flat top before he stopped and turned. Miriam was at Adam's side, helping him from the saddle. The movement had started him bleeding. He looked over to Taggart. "I'll be all right," he said, and fainted.

Consuelo went to him quickly. "Let me," she said. And when Miriam hesitated, she added, *"Por favor?"*

Miriam stepped back a little. "All right, Connie," she said, and picked up her rifle again.

Taggart stood facing Shoyer. "There's plenty of them down there, but we're getting out. This could be a death trap."

"You'll go when I tell you," Shoyer replied. "We haven't a chance!"

"We're going out of here now, and we're taking that chance," Taggart said. "They'll be sending up a smoke within the next few minutes and have half the Apaches in Arizona coming down on us. You do what you please. I'm taking them out of here, and I'm taking their gold with them."

The two men faced each other in the hot afternoon sun. For the first time Pete Shoyer saw Swante Taggart as he was, as something other than just another scalp to be taken in. He realized he was facing a tough and dangerous man . . . and a man whose side was right.

Taggart put it plain. "The gold is not yours, Shoyer. The woman is not yours. You make another stab at taking either and you're an outlaw."

"I've taken that step," Shoyer replied coolly. "I'm taking both the woman and the gold, only I'm taking it all. You had your chance. I told you to stay out of my way and I'd stay out of yours. . . . Well, you're wanting trouble. You asked for it by staying on . . . now you've got it."

"Why, sure!" Taggart replied. "I'm ready for it. Make your move."

"Stop it!" Miriam had her rifle on them. "The first one who touches a gun I'll kill. We've got Indians to fight."

"And I'll kill the other one." Stark was sitting up, pistol in hand.

Taggart turned abruptly away and went to the mules, where he began tightening the loosened cinches. Pete Shoyer stared after him, his face dark and impassive, his eyes utterly cold.

"I'll kill you," he said conversationally. "I'll take your scalp back to New Mexico and collect on it."

Taggart ignored him. Stark switched to his own horse and Taggart mounted up. For a moment they glanced at each other.

"Look!" Miriam pointed.

A thin column of smoke was rising, and as it lifted, it broke.

Swante Taggart rode over the rim and started down the trail. The others followed, and they went fast. They were almost halfway down before the firing began. A shot rang out and Stark fired almost as the flame stabbed from behind a rock, and he shot perfectly. An Apache lunged out from behind the rock, tumbled over and over, then came up shooting and three bullets nailed him as one.

Riding hard, Taggart hit the brush and, turning, blasted three shots along the face of the forest from where some of the firing had come.

Consuelo held a rifle and rode like an Indian, straight up and shooting. They plunged into the trail toward Nugget Wash, driving the pack animals ahead of them. Shoyer brought up the rear, firing at intervals. One of the pack animals was bleeding badly, the blood scattering along the trail.

Taggart pushed on, levering a shell into his Winchester as an Indian leaned from the rocks to get a better shot, and holding the rifle in one hand like a pistol, Taggart fired, splashing rock splinters in the Apache's face. He jerked back, exposing his body, and Consuelo shot into it. The Indian let go and tumbled down the slope to land sprawling beside the trail.

It was a wild ride down the narrow trail which plunged down the mountainside and into Nugget Wash. Coming briefly into the open, Taggart saw three smokes ahead of them, and he turned abruptly and left the trail. He climbed out of the wash, the others following and driving the pack animals. One of the animals made the shoulder above the trail, staggered on, and then fell.

Taggart was down swiftly and slashing at the pack saddle. Jerking it free he tumbled the saddle, gold and all, into a narrow crevice in the rocks and shoved gravel and rocks over it. It would look like debris which had fallen from their passing.

He pointed to a slash of white in the red rock above the spot. "There's your mark! Come and get it in better times!"

111

Then he led them west from the trail, working his way through rough and broken country. Sometimes he was up ahead, sometimes he was driving the pack animals.

But they were not clear of trouble. Suddenly an Apache broke from the brush close by and sprang at Taggart, knife in hand. It was Stark who killed him, firing three fast shots that knocked him from Taggart's shoulder.

The Indians came out of the brush in a swarm and for a moment there was a mêlée of plunging horses and blazing guns. Taggart wheeled his horse and drove the plunging pack mules into the attackers and, charging one Indian, shot almost into his face. Stark had pulled off to one side where, sitting coolly in his saddle, with his weight shifted to his right stirrup, he fired his pistol methodically.

Pete Shoyer charged with the mules and rode into the attacking Indians, rifle blasting. One Apache he caught with a lifting rifle muzzle and the sight of the rifle ripped a gash under the man's chin, tearing it to the bone and showering him with blood. Following through, Shoyer struck him with a swinging rifle butt and brought the man down.

Consuelo, all her fear gone now that the fight was upon them, was firing like a man and riding like a demon.

The fight could have lasted no more than a minute or two, and then it broke off suddenly and they were charging down the trail again. Taggart thumbed cartridges into his rifle, and reloaded his pistol. Their horses were lathered and they had lost another pack mule, this one the one with the supplies.

At a run they charged across the ground, riding over a rough and broken area that, under ordinary circumstances, none of them would have dreamed of crossing at more than a walk. Taggart still led, pushing toward Pinal Creek. There was a ranch somewhere on Pinal Creek, he believed, and it might give them temporary shelter.

Pete Shoyer closed in on Consuelo. "Come on!" he said. "Let's get out of here! We'll take one mule and ride!"

"No," she said, "I stay with my husband."

For an instant Shoyer's face was savage. "You don't pull that on me!" he said. "*Come on!*"

He grabbed at her arm, and like a striking adder she stabbed at him with a knife, but he jerked away just in time. His face was still and hard, his eyes cold. "All right," he said. "I'll kill you for that."

Consuelo rode away from him and pulled up alongside Stark, who seemed not to notice Shoyer. The gunman held his horse, and then abruptly he swung away from them and started away across the hills. Grouped and silent, they watched him go, but nobody called after him, nor spoke of him.

When he topped out on the rise, he drew rein and they saw him there, darkly ominous against the red sun of the ending day. Miriam, staring at him, felt a shudder of apprehension.

He was for a moment as if suspended there, as if he were part of the sunset, and then he was gone and the horizon was empty.

Chapter 13

Swante Taggart led the pack train into Globe with his Winchester across the saddle in front of him. He sat straight in the saddle, with his hat pulled down and his moccasined feet thrust into the stirrups. The horse he rode was beat, and even the Missouri hard-tails were walking with heads low, slogging it along the trail into town.

Miriam rode behind him, carrying her own rifle and followed by the mules. Bringing up the rear were Consuelo and Adam Stark.

The town of Globe was a huddle of shacks and tents on the east bank of Pinal Creek, an isolated town whose isolation was its own protection. Every citizen had at least one gun within reach at any given moment. They expected an Apache attack at any time. Freighters brought wagon trains in from Silver City at intervals, and there was some communication with Tucson and Prescott.

The arrival of battered and bloody pack trains or

freight wagons was not an unusual sight in Globe during those first years of its rugged life, and only a few citizens turned to look at the pack train that headed for the Wells Fargo office. Those few were seasoned mining men who knew a thing or two about pack trains and the comparative weight of various packs. These were obviously heavy, and heavy packs usually meant gold.

Leaving both girls and Stark himself sitting guard over the gold, Taggart pushed open the door of the nearest saloon. He stepped into the room, a tall, unshaven figure with a bloody bandage on his left arm and a rifle in his right hand. At the bar he asked the bartender, "Where's the Wells Fargo man?"

The bartender, a bald-pated man with red cheeks and a thick mustache, jerked his head toward a man down the bar. Then he called out, "Joe! Gent askin' for Wells Fargo!"

All heads turned, measuring Taggart with cool eyes. Joe was a short, squarely built man with a square, competent face. "What can I do for you?"

"Deposit," Taggart said.

They walked out together, and one man followed them to the door. At a comment over his shoulder, several others congregated to watch the mules unloaded, then drifted across the street to see what went on.

Taggart was standing on the stoop of the express office and he stopped them at mid-road. "Hold it!" he said. "No offense, but this is private business."

"What you got in those sacks?"

"Lay-overs to catch meddlers," Taggart said, using an answer he remembered from his grandmother.

"Is that gold?"

"Snakes," he said, "and Apache heads. We skinned our snakes back up the line a ways, and any of you boys hitting the trail tomorrow may find trouble around. I don't think we were friendly enough."

One by one the sacks were carried inside while Taggart stood on guard. Slowly, the spectators drifted back into the saloon, where all news eventually was passed out. The agent would be back in a little while and then they would know what was in those sacks. He'd tell them . . . he was a man who loved a good story.

114

Only it didn't work out that way. When the last of the gold was measured out and sacked up again, and receipts given for it, Joe hurried to close up. As he started to walk back toward the saloon Taggart dropped a rifle barrel across in front of him and Adam Stark smiled and said, "Not tonight. Tonight you're our guest."

"But I've got a bottle over there!" Joe said.

"You stick with us. You'll have all you can drink, on us."

Protesting, he was ushered across the street and into a shack that advertised BEDS. Stark promptly bought out the house. Then he sent out for a few bottles and, handing a bottle to Joe, he said, "You wanted to drink, go ahead and get drunk, get stone drunk, dead drunk. But if you try to leave this place before stage time tomorrow you'll be able to feed yourself through the hole in the other side of your head."

"Now look here!" Joe objected. "I—!"

"Drink," Stark replied.

They sat out the night, the two girls dozing in chairs near the wall, Taggart and Stark trading places on watch. At daylight Taggart stood on the stoop and watched the pale light find its way down the gray street and along the shabby, wind-worn buildings. There was no sign of Pete Shoyer.

Miriam came out to join him. "You think he'll come back?" she said, reading his thoughts.

"He'll come."

"What time is the stage due?"

"Shortly after ten, and we'll ride out with it. You two inside, Stark and I alongside. He can sell the mules, they're at a premium here."

"And then?"

"Tucson."

Miriam was silent. And after that? Swante Taggart was not speaking of the after time, for he did not know. No man knew what would happen then. He seemed so sure, so confident, but she knew what a bullet might do.

Most skilled gunfighters avoided each other, she knew that. There were occasional meetings between them, but they preferred to avoid trouble . . . there was too much of a chance that both men would be killed.

Somewhere a door banged shut and a windlass began to creak. A rooster crowed, and then there was silence. A dog trotted into the dusty street and lay down to roll.

"A man comes a long way," Taggart said, "to get where I am now."

"Shoyer is a dangerous man."

"It was not that I was thinking of." He paused. "I was thinking of you. You're a lot of woman, Miriam, the kind a man would want."

"A girl waits a long time, too."

A lone horseman rode down the street and dismounted in front of the saloon. He was a stranger.

He went up on the stoop and banged on the saloon door, but there was no response. Turning, he saw the two in front of the sign that said BEDS. "Where can a man get a bite to eat?" he yelled. "I'm hongry!"

Taggard pointed with the Winchester at the squat little building with glass in its one window. It was no more than sixty feet away, but the man swung into his saddle to ride the distance.

"Adam is grateful to you," Miriam said. "Without you we would never have gotten through."

"Without me you might never have had any trouble. I brought trouble to you."

"No."

The strange rider had interrupted their conversation and Miriam wanted to get back on the right trail with Taggart, but she was not sure how to do it. She had always been outspoken with men, more direct than a woman should be, but now she could find no words, she could just look at him foolishly, feeling very young and suddenly awkward. She must look a sight. How could any man be romantic with a girl who looked as she must look?

Adam Stark came to the door, followed by Consuelo. Somehow the Mexican girl had contrived to make herself look lovely, and Miriam stared at her enviously, wondering how she could do it so easily.

"He's out cold." Stark jerked his head toward the express agent inside. "I say we load up the stage and take it out ourselves."

"There'll be a driver."

116

"We'll need him. I won't feel safe until this stuff is on deposit in Tucson."

"Wells Fargo are responsible right now."

"Anyway, we're making sure." Stark glanced quickly at Taggart. "You're with me, aren't you?"

"As far as Tucson? Yes."

He was going on then. Miriam tried not to show her feelings. He was going to leave, after all this. After all what? There had been nothing between them . . . neither of them had said much, only back there in the night they had talked a bit, but what did that matter? What did it really matter?

But the thought of Swante Taggart troubled her. What kind of a life was this for anyone? Eating no regular meals, sleeping anywhere at all, nobody to do for him. Like that arm . . . blood all over it and the flesh cut deep by a bullet, and he had said nothing about it until she found him bandaging it himself.

A few people were moving around now. They left the BEDS and strolled across to the eating house, and while Adam and Consuelo ate, Taggart stood outside with Miriam.

"Always wanted a place with a few cows," he said. "Life like that is mighty lonely."

"I suppose so."

"A man has to live on his grass. Mostly it's far from anywhere . . . no near neighbors, nobody to talk to. It's a wonder a man like that ever finds him a woman."

"If a woman loved a man she would live anywhere, anywhere at all."

"A man who loves a woman wants to give her things. He wants to pretty her up . . . dresses and such things. A man on a ranch may not make much for three, four years. Maybe longer. He doesn't have much to offer."

He stared gloomily across the street. "Best thing a man can do is keep traveling. Keeps him from getting ideas. A man settles down he stagnates, he dries up, loses all his get-up-and-go."

Stark and Consuelo came out of the restaurant. The other two started in, but Consuelo stopped Miriam. "I was a fool," she said. "I am sorry."

"We're all fools part of the time. Some of us most of

the time. Men just as much as women, and some of them are as stubborn as any mule-headed bronc."

Taggart started in the door, then flushing, he stepped back and held the door open for her.

There were three tables covered with a kind of slick cloth that Taggart had not seen before, and a waiter in a smeared apron crossed to take their order. "Ain't seen a egg this week," he said, "not until this morning. I got three left."

"Mr. Taggart will have them. I will have whatever else you have."

"I got meat. I got beef meat, deer meat, hog meat, and some mountain sheep meat. I can recommend any of it."

"Take the horns off a sheep and bring him in," Taggart suggested, "and you scramble those eggs and split them two ways. Miss Stark will have half of them."

The waiter stared owlishly from one to the other. "Now listen to that! You two are sure formal with each other. What you think this is, Boston?"

He waddled away and they looked at each other and laughed. Miriam felt herself blushing and looked at her plate. Her fingers were twisted together in her lap, and suddenly she was embarrassed before this man in whose company she had been for days . . . and nights.

In one way, you could even say they had slept together. At the thought she blushed again, worse than before. It was nothing like that. Only they were together, and they had slept. A little, anyway.

They ate in silence. Swante Taggart was a man who appreciated food, and the coffee was just right, he decided. You could float a horse shoe in it. Dump in plenty of coffee, wet it down, and boil it. That was the way to make it. Best coffee was always made in an old tin pail.

The waiter came over as they finished eating. He had a huge apple pie which he placed on the table. "Honor of the occasion," he said. "First time I had two such good-lookin' women in here as you an' that Mex gal that was just in here."

He stared at Miriam and then at Taggart. "You and him sure are lucky. Ain't but three single women in Globe right now, and one of them is old enough to be Andy Jackson's grandmother."

When they went outside the stage rolled into town. The relief driver came out of a shack stuffing his shirt into his pants with one hand and carrying a gun belt in the other. "Wonder they wouldn't wake a man up," he growled. He glanced at the Starks, at Taggart and Miriam. "You passengers?"

Without waiting for an answer, he watched them hook the traces of the fresh team. They looked wild and eager, bronco mules and bad ones.

Then he crossed to the BEDS and shook the snoring agent down for his keys. He wakened him, but without waiting for him or expecting him to follow, he crossed to the station and opened the door and unlocked the big iron safe.

With Taggart helping, the gold was loaded. The two girls got in and Stark waited outside. Taggart put the last sack into the boot.

An oldish man with a yellowed mustache appeared and climbed up to the seat. He was the express messenger. He seated himself and cradled a shotgun across his knees, directing a hard look at Taggart and Stark. Taggart stepped into the saddle and Stark mounted up. The stage driver cracked his whip and yelled, and the mules lunged into their harness as if the devil had lit fires under them. They took off for the south.

It was a quiet ride, those first few miles. Taggart and Stark were tired after the long night with little sleep, and the sun was warm. They dozed in the saddle, roused themselves to look around, and then dozed again. Gradually, they fell back.

The road at first followed the bed of Pinal Creek, shaded by oak, sycamore, and cottonwood, then it wound upward through the green Pinal Mountains. Many tiny streams fell from rocky crevices, sometimes tumbling a hundred feet. Finally they came down to the valley where Dripping Springs Station was located. Beyond lay the barren, rugged slopes of the Mescals, red and russet in the evening sun.

The stage rolled up to the long, low station and came to a halt. A few minutes later, Adam Stark, stiff from his bruised and battered muscles, rode up, and behind him came Swante Taggart.

Taggart swung down. Suddenly he realized he was dead tired. The excitement and pressure of the weeks past was catching up with him, and he leaned heavily against the horse for a minute or two before he shook off his weariness and went about stabling his horse.

There was a shed stable here, and corrals. He led the steeldust to a stall and tied him there, and forked hay into the manger.

Miriam had climbed down from the stage and was standing alone near it. Consuelo had gone inside, and Adam was talking to the mustached express messenger.

The sun was just going down; the sky was bright and the air clear. Somewhere out through the last of the trees, a quail called. And when Pete Shoyer stepped around the corner of the stage station Swante Taggart saw him at once.

They faced each other across a hundred feet and there was no doubt in the mind of either that this was the moment. Swante Taggart had a fleeting thought that it could not have been at a worse time for him, tired as he was, but he aware this was it.

He could hear water falling somewhere, and the horses munching hay in the mangers. A large, drowsy fly buzzed somewhere nearby. These sounds seemed strangely clear. A horse stamped and Miriam turned slowly, her eyes on Taggart. Then she stifled a gasp as she saw Pete Shoyer. Adam Stark appeared on the porch and with him was Consuelo.

Shoyer had taken a step forward. "I'm takin' you in, Taggart!" he said loudly.

"Why, come and take me then," Taggart replied, and watched Shoyer come toward him.

Then suddenly Shoyer's head thrust forward and his right hand dropped, but as it dropped Taggart took a fast step to the right and drew as he moved. He felt the heavy gun swing up, felt the jolt of the shot, and then another jolt as he was spun around.

He started to fall, but stiffened his knees and fired a second time. Shoyer seemed hazy, a difficult target. Another shot struck him and a third kicked up dust at his feet. Taggart ran three light, fast steps to the right and fired again.

Then he fell. He smelled dust and blood and knew he was down. He heard the blast of a gun. Dust was kicked into his face and he rolled over into a sitting position and, lifting his six-shooter, he shot into Shoyer's body, firing once, then again.

A bullet *whiffed* past Taggart's face and he began to thumb shells into his gun, and then he got to his knees and started to rise. His leg buckled under him and he fell again, feeling a bullet pass him as he went down. And then he shot upward from a prone position, rolled over and got up, all the way this time.

There was blood on his face and he could taste blood in his mouth, and he felt a strange weakness in his body. He held his gun ready as he looked around slowly, trying to place Shoyer, but he could not find him. Miriam was grasping his arm and crying, and he was trying to shake her off, sure she would be killed.

Then he saw Pete Shoyer. The gunman was sprawled on the adobe soil near the corner of the stage station. Taggart lifted his gun.

"It's all right," Stark was saying. "He's dead."

"Who killed him then?" Taggart demanded. "This was my fight. I—"

He felt himself slipping; he tried to lift his gun. But as he fell he heard Adam Stark say, "Why, you killed him, man, and a good job it was, too."

There was an arm under his head and he heard someone sobbing. He felt his shirt torn open, and someone else was tearing his pants leg. He wished they would go away. Besides, this was the last pair of pants he had.

He heard himself speaking. "Adam," he said, "I would like to ask the hand of your sister in marriage."

There was a moment then when he was aware of nothing, and when he opened his eyes later they were all around him and he was on a table in the stage station.

"I asked a question," he said.

"And I answered," Miriam said, "I give myself to you."

"This is between men," Taggart replied. "It was your brother I asked."

"Why, yes," Adam said, "she could go far and not find so much of a man. I'll give her to you on condition you join us on the ranch we'll find somewhere near Tucson. We will need a man who knows cows."

Taggart turned his head stiffly. His skull throbbed heavily and he knew he must have been hit there, too, but he felt very much alive. "All right then," he said to Miriam, "I accept your acceptance. We will be married then, and if there is any beauty after this that I can bring to you, it shall be yours."

He was delirious, he decided, but it was not a bad way to be. He was delirious or he was happy, or he was both, and he put his head back on the table.

"Here's his gun," somebody said. "I've put his horse in the stable."

His horse and his gun, he thought. It was all he had when he rode up to the canyon of the chapel, and now he still had his horse and his gun, but he also had a woman and a friend.